The
KISSING
GAME

AIDAN CHAMBERS

Amulet Books
New York

The KISSING GAME

Short Stories

ACKNOWLEDGEMENTS

'The Tower' first appeared in *A Haunt of Ghosts* edited by Aidan Chambers, Bodley Head, 1987. 'The Kissing Game' first appeared in *Love All* edited by Aidan Chambers, Bodley Head, 1988. 'The Scientific Approach' first appeared in *Rush Hour*, Vol. Three, edited by Michael Cart, Delacorte Press, 2005. The short dialogues owe their inspiration to *One Million Tiny Plays About Britain* by Craig Taylor, Bloomsbury, 2009.

Library of Congress Cataloging-in-Publication Data:
Chambers, Aidan.
The kissing game : short stories / Aidan Chambers.
p. cm.
ISBN 978-0-8109-9716-5 (alk. paper)
I. Title.
PR6053.H285K57 2011
823'.914—dc22
2010032947

Text copyright © 2011 Aidan Chambers
Title type and ornaments by Jessica Hische
Book design by Melissa Arnst

Pages 151 and 154: From *Happy Moscow* by Andrey Platonov, translated by Robert and Elizabeth Chandler, published by Harvill Press. Reprinted by permission of The Random House Group Ltd.

Printed and bound in the United States of America
10 9 8 7 6 5 4 3 2 1

Amulet Books are available at special discounts when purchased in quantity for premiums and promotions as well as fundraising or educational use. Special editions can also be created to specification. For details, contact specialmarkets@abramsbooks.com or the address below.

115 West 18th Street
New York, NY 10011
www.abramsbooks.com

Contents

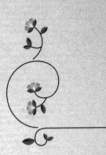

Cindy's Day Out

ENOUGH! SHE SAID TO HERSELF.

That's it. I've had enough.

No more 'Cindy, get me this. Cindy, get me that. Where are you, Cindy?'

No more 'Cindy' either.

Today is mine.

Today is for me.

Not Cindy.

But *me*.

Ursula Oracod.

Today other people will do this for me and that for me and everything I want for me and do it when I please.

The middle of three sisters, one nineteen, the other sixteen, 'her' seventeen and the odd one out. Not lively and clever like Imogen, the oldest. Not sexily beautiful and bursting with confidence like

Beatrice, the youngest. But—so they all said, sisters, mother, father, even her grandparents—plain, simple, ordinary, entirely unmemorable Ursula. The one whose name visitors forgot—and then called 'her' Cindy because that's what 'her' sisters called her. The one whose only feature people remembered, if they remembered anything about 'her', were 'her' sticking out ears, which she tried to hide by an elaborate exercise with a curling iron.

There was of course the other reason for being the odd one out. But that was unmentionable.

Her sisters were not the only ones who used her like a servant, worse in fact, like a slave (at least servants are paid). Her mother was just as bad. Now, since her seventeenth birthday, leaving her to do the weekly supermarket shopping on her own. 'Here's the credit card, darling, and some cash for a taxi home. I wish I had the time but I don't. A client to see all day. And this week, don't forget the Tropicana fruit juice Beatrice likes.'

Her father wasn't quite as bad. Sometimes, he even stuck up for her, and told whoever was ordering her about to try doing it for themselves for once. But he always received the same reply: 'But, Dad, I'm in such a hurry and Cindy doesn't mind, do you, Cindy?' No reply was awaited. And with three women against him, her father shut up. There being the unmentionable to avoid as well.

So Ursula was the family runabout, treated as such ever since she was thirteen when the unmentionable had been revealed. She wouldn't have put up with it, if she were as funny as Imogen or as quick-thinking as Beatrice. But she'd never been able to give as good as she got in either repartee or arguments. Nor was she any match for Imogen's knowledge of just about everything. (When and how did she learn so much? She never seemed to spend any time studying.) Besides, Imogen and Beatrice were best friends. So: odd one out again.

But today she had finally had enough.

Luckily, it was the summer holidays. Imogen had gone off to visit her latest boyfriend. (Never matching up to her required standard of body and brain, her boyfriends tended to last a month at most.) Beatrice was still in bed pursuing her beauty sleep and would not put in an appearance before midday at the earliest. Her parents were at work.

There was a summer outfit of Imogen's, a red top and forest-brown jeans by Karen Millen, that Ursula really liked but had been told by all and sundry was 'too sophisticated for you, not your style *at all*.'

She went to Imogen's room, found the outfit in Imogen's abundant wardrobe that smelt of her favourite scent, Flower by Kenzo, carried it to her own room and put it on.

There is justice in the world! It fit perfectly, touching in the right places and loose everywhere else. Till now she had thought she was too big around the hips to fit into anything of Imogen's, unless it was of the ultra sloppy fashion.

Next, the question of shoes. Neither her mother's nor Imogen's fit her. Beatrice had a pair of Geox Respiras she'd love to wear, and would fit, but they were in Beatrice's room, and asleep though Beatrice might be, going into her room would inevitably wake her. Ursula had read that when you see birds standing on one leg it means the half of the bird on the side of the raised leg was asleep, but the half on which the bird was standing was awake. She wondered if something like that might be true of Beatrice. Only half of her asleep at a time. Besides, if Beatrice was anything, she was territorial and possessive. She always knew when anybody had been in her precious room, even if you didn't touch any of her precious things. As for taking something, no matter how trivial, the result was a tsunami of recriminations it was best to avoid.

She'd have to make do with her own shoes. She chose a pair of black heels that were always comfortable and made her feel light on her feet.

She showered, dried her hair, put on a new bra and panties, did her best to spray-rigid her hair over her ears, and then put on Imogen's outfit and her own heels.

Looking at the result in the mirror, she was slightly irritated to find that the only part of her that felt comfortable was her feet. As for the rest, it wasn't Ursula. But it wasn't Cindy either, and today this was all that mattered.

II

The High Street wasn't busy.

Too early in the day.

Where should she start?

One of the department stores would offer the best range. She wasn't sure what range she wanted or what she was going to do. Except that whatever it was, someone else would be doing the doing.

In Camden House she wandered past the jewellery section (she wasn't in the mood for that just yet), and then the sections for Armani and Gucci and Prada, all tempting to poke about in, but kept for later when there'd be more people and she wouldn't feel so conspicuous. At the moment every assistant she went by looked beady and ready to pounce on her.

Now the cosmetics section. Makeup wasn't her thing. She never bothered with it. Mainly because Imogen and Beatrice bothered so much with it. But maybe she ought to?

She paused to look at the range on the first counter. She liked the little round cakes ranked in neat black boxes like lozenges of paint in a painting box. They appealed because she'd always liked painting, even though she wasn't much good at it. For the same reason, she liked the brushes you were meant to use to apply the makeup.

An assistant came up to her, a middle-aged woman in a tight black dress and white scarf, precisely made up and with hair that looked as if it wouldn't move even in a gale. A soldier in the battle for sales.

'Can I help you?' she asked with a smile.

'I was wondering,' Ursula said, summoning all her determination to be the one in charge, 'I was wondering which foundation would be the best for me. Maybe the sort that has an illuminating factor in it?'

She surprised herself. She had never uttered the words 'illuminating factor' before. She'd read them in one of Imogen's fashion magazines, and the words popped out of her mouth as if said many times.

'Let's see,' the assistant said, peering closely at Ursula's face. 'Lancôme do a good range.'

She took a sample from a cupboard and laid it on the glass of the counter.

Ursula stared at it, not now as confident as a moment ago and not sure what to do or say next.

'You can try it, if you like,' the assistant said. 'The testers are here.'

Ursula hesitated. What she wanted was someone else to try it for her.

'Is it your day off?' the assistant asked.

'Yes,' Ursula said.

'The sort of job you need to look your best, I expect?'

'I . . . help out with a family.'

'An au pair?'

'That sort of thing.'

'I was an au pair once,' the assistant said, 'when I was about your age. It was hard work. I really needed my day off, when I didn't have to think about doing anything for anybody but myself.'

'Yes,' Ursula said. 'That's right.'

The assistant waited a moment before saying, 'Why not consult our Lancôme representative, if you aren't sure? She's here this morning and I think she has a bit of time before her first client. I'm sure she'd be happy to help.'

Ursula hesitated, wondering about the cost.

The assistant leaned towards her, and giving her a complicit smile said quietly, 'There'd be no charge, of course. And no obligation to buy. It's one of our services.'

Ursula smiled back.

'All right then. Thanks.'

'Follow me,' the assistant said, and led her to an area where there were a couple of high chairs and mirrors lit like the mirrors in theatre dressing rooms. She introduced her to an older woman, also in the uniform black dress with white scarf, who asked her to sit down.

The light was so bright and the mirrors so sharp they showed every pore and fleck in Ursula's face, and seemed to exaggerate the fright of her hair, a sight from which she turned her eyes in embarrassment.

The Lancôme lady spoke with a strong accent, rasping her *rrrr*s, which Ursula decided was French.

'*Je parle français aussi*,' Ursula said, in a showing-off sort of voice which she used when feeling defensive, and always regretted afterwards.

'*Très bien. Donc*, what mademoiselle rrrequires is a good cleansing.'

Ursula was about to say 'I had a shower before I came out,' but this time she held her tongue.

And so the makeup makeover began.

At first, Ursula was on edge, never having been the object of minute close inspection before, except by her dentist, and that wasn't the same thing at all.

Soon, she settled back into comfort, enjoying the business of being pampered, 'cleansed', 'prepared' and applied with foundation by finger, and eyeliner by pencil, and blush by brush, and then it came to the lipstick.

'Which would mademoiselle prefer? Lancôme L'Absolu Rrrouge Rrrendez-Vous, verrry nutritious, or the Colour Fever Daring Rrrose, verrry rrred? L'Absolu Rrrouge I think would be nice, does mademoiselle agree, *hein*? The Colour Fever is too too rrred for mademoiselle. L'Absolu Rrrouge is subtle. And will bring out the colour of her pretty eyes.'

Her eyes had never before been called pretty.

She was so pleased she heard herself say, 'I'll trust your choice. You're the expert.'

'*Merci*, mademoiselle. L'Absolu Rrrouge, then. *Bon*.'

Her face finished, the assistant who had helped her first was called over. There was clucking and compliments and exclamations of '*La différence!*' from the Lancôme lady, and 'Beautiful!' from the other one.

But then the first assistant turned to the Lancôme lady, 'The hair?'

'I am *not* a hairstylist,' said the Lancôme lady rather sharply.

'Still,' the other one said. 'Maybe something could be done to help. A pity not to . . .'

The Lancôme lady studied Ursula in the mirror and began fluffing and flicking about.

'*Oui*, yes, well, *peut-être* . . .'

'You could manage something,' the other said.

'Something better than *this* anyway,' the makeup expert said with Gallic scorn. 'Mademoiselle's style is certainly dérrrangé.'

The other assistant went off to attend to a customer and the Lancôme lady began flummering with Ursula's hair.

An hour and a half had gone by when all was done.

Ursula stood up and considered herself in the mirror, turning this way and that, the Lancôme lady standing back, hands clasped in the manner of a nun.

She was amazed.

Was this herself?

Was this *her*?

Was this Ursula Oracod?

The question blurred her mind and her vision.

She liked it and she didn't like it.

It was her and it wasn't her.

III

She got up and left the store in a daze of confusion.

On the street she stopped for a moment and people swerved by her.

She tried to think whether she had thanked the makeup specialist, but couldn't remember. She did remember that the assistant who had helped her first had smiled at her as she passed the cosmetics counter and said, 'You look lovely. A new woman.'

A new woman?

Was she?

She didn't feel new.

She felt like Ursula Oracod dressed up to play a part in a film.

Thinking this, she only half-heard the wolf whistle. Never having been whistled at before, she paid no attention.

Then she heard it again and a rough male voice shouting from across the road, 'Over here, darlin'!'

She looked.

The building opposite was caged in scaffolding.

The wolf whistle again. From somewhere on the scaffolding.

She saw him. A builder wearing a yellow hard hat, a mucky white T-shirt and jeans, with tools hanging from a belt round his waist. He was leaning on a rail and grinning at her.

When he saw her looking at him, he made an obscene gesture with his tongue, laughed, and shouted, 'Any time, sweetheart, any time!'

All she could think of was that Imogen and Beatrice would have snapped out an amusing put-down without a second's pause. But she could think of nothing, only felt humiliated and embarrassed.

She set off aimlessly down the street, wanting to get out of earshot of the man on the scaffold before he could shout anything more, and from passersby who were staring at her and grinning.

She passed a Costa coffee shop. Thought that having a coffee would be a comfort, turned back and went in.

There was a queue of six or seven. Two girls not much older than herself were serving. As usual chattering to each other about their night out last night, taking hardly any notice of the customers.

When it came to her turn there was the usual robotic mantra: kind of coffee required, large, small or medium, take out or have in, and anything else?

She ordered a café latte medium. And when it came to paying riffled in her bag for the money, which, as usual, had somehow burrowed its way to the bottom and hid among her other stuff.

'Let me,' said a man next to her, who was paying for his own coffee, and handed over the money before she had time to object.

'I've got it,' she said, still scrabbling.

'My pleasure,' the man said, picking up her coffee as well as his own.

She was going to object and say no, when she remembered her rule for today. Other people must do things for her, not her for others. If this man wanted to pay, let him. No skin off her nose, after all. She hadn't asked him to.

'Over there?' the man said, nodding towards a table with two seats by the window.

She followed him because there was no option and sat down.

He looked about thirty, blue suit, white shirt, red, blue and green striped tie, loosened at the neck and the top button of his shirt undone. He had a hard face, tight lips, spiky nose, iron-grey eyes and black hair in crinkly little waves. One thing she didn't like was hair in crinkly little waves.

'Having your coffee break?' the man asked when they had taken their first drinks.

'No,' she said, the irritation caused by his hair sharpening her voice.

'Day off?'

'Sort of.'

She looked out of the window to stop herself from looking at him.

They took another drink as if in rehearsed unison.

'I work in an insurance office across the road,' he said.

'Really?' she said, automatic politeness making her look at him but trying not to show interest.

'I know. Dull.'

'Is it?'

'Well paid, though.'

'That's something.'

'Enough to run an SLK 200.'

'Sorry?'

'A Mercedes-Benz. Two-seater. Vario roof. Compressor. Cruise control. Silver. Very fast.'

She was meant to be impressed.

'Is that so?' she said as flatly as she could.

'Not interested in cars?'

'No.'

More coffee.

'Ever had a run in a Merc sports?'

'Never.'

'You'd enjoy it.'

She said nothing.

'Just name the day and time.'

Imogen would have told him to get lost because of his brazen approach. Beatrice would have accepted and then dumped him, because she was up for anything and would have liked telling about it afterwards. Typically, Ursula didn't know what to say. Half pleased that this man wanted to pick her up; half annoyed by his cheap pass. Not to mention his hair. And thought again, as when she was wolf whistled, that it was only because of the way she looked today that this was happening. It had never happened before, not here where she'd been a few times, not anywhere.

'Got to go,' she said, and stood up.

'Don't know what you're missing,' he said. There

was a hardness in his tone now that resembled the hardness of his face.

'Nor you,' she heard herself say just as hard and quite unthought, which made her smile with pleasure at herself. 'Thanks for the coffee,' she added, and left.

Now what? Where now?

Aimlessness was not her. She disliked being without a plan. Each morning, when she woke, she spent a few minutes going over what she would do that day. It was her sisters and her mother interrupting her plans by asking her to do this or that that annoyed her more than doing things for them. If their wants had been part of her plans she'd never have minded.

But today she had set off without any plan in mind. And now she was feeling the miss of it.

Then she remembered there was something she wanted to do. Borrow from the library a new book by one of her favourite authors, Griselda Walsh.

She crossed the road and walked down the High Street to the central library. Here she was in familiar territory. She'd spent many hours doing homework and preparing for exams away from her sisters' noise and their demands. And anyway, she liked being surrounded by books. They were comforting and stimulating. She felt more at home among them than she did anywhere else except in her own room.

As soon as she entered the library she felt better. Felt she was herself again.

She made straight for the section of 'New Books'. A librarian she'd seen often before was there, tidying the shelves, a young man with a shaggy little beard whisping from his chin. She had always wanted to clip it off because she thought it was silly and he'd look better without it. She guessed he grew it to try and look older, but even with it he still looked like a lanky boy. He said nothing to her, didn't even look, as she scanned the shelves, but then, he never had said anything or paid her any attention, even when he had checked out books for her, except for the usual routine questions.

When she couldn't find what she wanted, she turned to him and said, 'Is *The Lover's Inspection* by Griselda Walsh in yet?'

The librarian looked at her—looked her over as if she were a new book cover would be more accurate— smiled—which was also a first—and said, 'We put six copies out this morning and they're gone already.'

'Rats!' she said, crestfallen. 'You're sure there's none left?'

'She's very popular at the minute,' he said.

'She's one of my favourites,' she said.

'There's copies of her earlier titles,' he said. 'I can show you.'

'I know where they are,' she said. 'And I've read them all.'

'Not your first time here, then?'

'No! What makes you think it is?'

'Haven't seen you before.'

She was about to protest and put him right, but held her tongue. Instead, she said tightly, 'Never mind. Forget it.'

And was turning to leave in a huff when the librarian said, 'Hang on a mo!'

She stopped and turned to him.

He looked round to make sure no one was in ear shot, moved close, and said hardly above a whisper, 'There's a copy in the office. I was keeping it to read before shelving it. I'll let you borrow it, if you like.'

The same thing again! Ursula thought. First a wolf whistle, then a coffee pickup, now him! He doesn't recognise me, even though he's seen me loads of times. But now that I'm all dolled up in someone else's flashy clothes, and with a face plastered with makeup, and hair sculptured in a style I would never have thought I'd be seen dead in, he turns on the charm and tries to bribe me with his condescension.

She felt like telling him to get stuffed. But why not let him play court in his pathetic way? she thought. Let him give me what I want. When — smiling to herself — he's not going to get what he wants!

So she said, coyly, 'Really? That's *so* great of you!'

***

The librarian returned with the book concealed in a Co-op plastic bag, and handed it to her with a wink, saying, 'Sorry about the bag. Bought a sandwich for my lunch and don't have anything else to put the book in.'

'No problem, thanks.'

'When you bring it back, can you give it to me similarly disguised?'

He was such a boy, passing secrets, she rather liked him after all, and smiled, saying, 'Sure. Of course.'

'I'm Martin, by the way. If I'm not around, ask for me.'

'I will. I'm Ursula.'

'And by the way,' he said up close again, 'did you know she's in town this morning?'

'Who?'

'Griselda Walsh.'

'Really? Where?'

'The Queen's Hotel. Her publishers are holding a sales conference for their reps and main booksellers. She's giving a talk about her next book. Her autobiography apparently. Due next year. I tried to get in, but no go for lowly librarians.'

'What a shame! At the Queen's?'

'Yes. Maybe you should go. Hang about in the lobby or something. Pretend to be waiting for somebody. You might see her. Get an autograph even.'

His boyish enthusiasm imbued her with unusual confidence.

'What a good idea!' she said, warming to him even more. 'Why not?'

'Wish I could come with you, but I'm on duty at the desk till five today.'

'I'll go. I'll try.'

'Come and tell me, if you see her.'

'I will.'

'Great! And enjoy the book.'

'Thanks again for letting me have it.'

'No prob, Ursula. Be seeing you.'

Have I made a new friend? Ursula wondered as she left the library and walked to the hotel. There's a turn-up for the book! A friend with a whispy beard. Well, at least he likes books and reading, which is more than I can say about some people I could name.

IV

The hotel lobby was bustling.

As she approached, Ursula was a touch nervous, less sure of herself than when Martin had suggested she go there. What would she say if one of the hotel staff accosted her? She was not familiar with hotels and their ways.

Inside the lobby was a large notice on a kind of easel displaying the message:

RODNOCK PUBLISHERS
SALES CONFERENCE
PRINCESS DIANA HALL

Ursula considered the situation.

The clock behind the reception desk said ten fifty.

When, she wondered, was Griselda Walsh giving her talk?

Maybe if she found her way to the Princess Diana Hall there'd be a notice showing the programme, or someone she could ask.

It wasn't difficult to see where the Hall was. A sign pointed the way up a staircase to the first floor. Various people were climbing the stairs, most of them carrying black linen bags with a logo on them in white and the word RODNOCK under it.

The people with the bags were coming out of the restaurant beside the lobby, no doubt from their morning break, to judge from the incense of coffee drifting out.

With a resurgence of confidence that surprised her,

Ursula followed the Rodnock crowd and arrived at an open area in front of the Hall. Tables with black covers draped over them, each with the Rodnock logo and name on them, lined one wall. On the tables were sheaves of paper, piles of what looked like catalogues, and copies of books displayed on little stands. Large posters of book covers were stuck on the wall behind the tables, and equally large pictures of the faces of what Ursula assumed must be writers, because she recognized a couple of them.

The largest poster of all, and most prominently displayed, was a book cover with the title *Words of My World* and the name Griselda Walsh. Beside this was an equally outsized photograph, head and shoulders, of Griselda Walsh, which Ursula recognised from the covers of the many Griselda Walsh books she'd read.

Slim young women in white blouses and smart tight jeans and black leather boots were standing behind the tables, talking across the tables to Rodnock-bag-carrying men in suits, who were apparently asking questions, but more likely, to judge by their body language, flirting with the young women, who wore smiles as tight and smart as their jeans.

Ursula was about to approach one of the tables to ask about the time of Griselda Walsh's talk, when the doors of the Hall opened and everyone started to go inside. Including the young women behind the tables.

At which Ursula's confidence slipped again. She remained where she was, wondering what to do next.

Within a couple of minutes everyone had gone inside and the doors of the Hall were closed again. Ursula felt conspicuously isolated standing alone in that large space. Instinct drew her to the tables, where she looked for the information she wanted among the documents littered there. She searched until she discovered a page with the Rodnock name and logo on it and the title *Sales Conference Programme*.

She scanned down till she came to:

11.00–11.25 Children's book editors present new books.

11.30–12.30 Griselda Walsh.

12.45–2.00 Lunch in the Prince William Restaurant.

She was considering this and wondering whether she had the nerve to hang around in the hope of seeing Griselda Walsh, when a voice behind her said, 'Have they gone in?'

She turned, to find Griselda Walsh a few feet away, unmistakably her, though somewhat older than the photograph displayed on the wall and on the covers of her books. Or, to be honest, more than somewhat. Her bobbed hair was white and her face, though well made-up, obviously wrinkled. She was slim, dressed in a sleek linen shift in autumn colours, a pale blue silk scarf loosely wound round her neck, the long ends drifting below her waist. But the effect was spoilt by a pair of reading glasses dangling from a silver chain round her neck.

Ursula was so taken aback she couldn't speak.

'Have they gone in?' Griselda Walsh repeated.

'Oh! Yes,' Ursula said. 'Yes—'

'Damn!' said Griselda Walsh. 'I thought I'd sit in on this session and assess the atmosphere and the audience before my session. Were you waiting for me?'

'Yes,' Ursula said, wondering how she knew.

'Jock said he'd make sure one of his girls was deputed to look after me. What's your name, dear?'

'Ursula,' Ursula said still in shock.

'My goodness, Ursula, but it's chilly down here, don't you think? Is it like this in the hall? I hate air-conditioning, don't you? It's always so cold and artificial. I never think it's real air at all, do you? You couldn't do something for me, could you? There's a linen jacket in my room. On the bed. I thought of wearing it and decided against at the last moment. Wrong! I never learn! Could you pop up and get it for me?' She approached Ursula, and handed her a piece of plastic like a credit card. 'Here's the key to my room. Five-four-five. I really would like to attend this session and rev myself up for the fray. I'll sit at the back so as not to disturb the current proceedings.

Could you bring the jacket to me? Very good of you, dear. You girls are always so efficient. And always so well turned out and such good-lookers. I don't know where Jock finds you all!'

She turned, went to the Hall door, opened it with elaborate caution, and slipped inside before Ursula could find her voice again.

What else could she do but as she'd been asked?

As she waited for the lift, she couldn't help laughing at being mistaken for one of Jock's girls — whoever Jock was — by the famous Griselda Walsh.

But when she got into the lift and pressed the button for the fifth floor the thought suddenly hit her: My favourite author, and what does she do? Calls me *dear* when she's never met me before and knows nothing about me, and treats me as Cindy just because she thinks I'm a member of somebody's staff! What a cheek! Just because she's a famous author. Because what is it she's doing, Miz Famous Walsh? She's treating me like *a Cindy*!

On the heels of this thought, admiration turned to bile.

I am *not* your *dear*, Ursula said to herself as the lift ascended. You do not know me. And I am *not* a *girl* on someone's bimbo staff! I will *not* be *Cindied* by *anyone*, not even by you, Miz Griselda Walsh! I am *Ursula Oracod* I will have you know, Miz Walsh. And today is my day out, when other people do things for me *not* me for them.

What's more, Miz Walsh, I hereby declare and swear I will never be anyone's *Cindy dear* ever again.

And I also hereby announce, she continued to herself as the lift doors opened, that you, Miz Griselda Walsh, are no longer one of my favourite authors. You were a favourite author of *Cindy* Oracod. Therefore you cannot be a favourite of *Ursula* Oracod.

She had trouble working out how to use the plastic key. In her irritation and nervousness, she put it into the little slot above the door handle the wrong way up, panicked for a second, till, trying again, she found it had to be a certain way round and up.

The door admitted her to a large room furnished with a bed the size of which would have accommodated all five of the Oracods at one go (not that she'd like that), a sitting area in front of a window the length of the outside wall, with a two-seater sofa in blue leather, a wide armchair, and a coffee table with a glass top on which was a vase of red and white roses, and a large tray bearing the remains of what must have been Miz Walsh's breakfast. (Not that she could have eaten much, as there were slices of toast in a rack, half a jug of orange juice, and an assortment of little bottles of jam and marmalade left untouched.) On the wall opposite the bed was a desk with files and a laptop on it, a mirror on the wall behind it, and next to the mirror a black flat-screen TV. On the wall above the bed was a picture of a seascape. A built-in wardrobe with sliding mirror doors occupied the little entrance hall, opposite which was a door standing open into a bathroom tiled in cream marble, a round hand basin with gold taps set into a mahogany stand on which were bottles and other toilet items and a considerable quantity of what Ursula assumed must be Miz Walsh's makeup, all of this reflected in a wall-length mirror. Opposite the hand basin was a deep bath and a separate shower cubicle and against the far wall a lavatory. Thick-looking white towels were draped from rails on the wall beside the basin.

She had never seen a room so sumptuous, except in magazines of course.

The author's linen jacket was on the bed.

Ursula picked it up and went back down to the first floor.

Ursula hesitated outside the Hall. The last thing she wanted was to be noticed and found out.

She opened the door a crack. The room was in semi-darkness. She could see over the heads of the audience a PowerPoint projected onto a screen at the front and a young woman in a black business suit standing at a lectern to the side of the screen, her voice amplified through loudspeakers.

'It is *such* a *sweet* story,' she was saying. 'The *breakthrough* for this author we've been waiting for. It'll sell like hotcakes, I promise!'

At which the audience broke into applause.

Ursula spotted Miz Walsh's white hair. She was in the back row only a few steps from the door.

Ursula took her chance while the audience was applauding to slip in, hand the linen jacket over the author's shoulder, drop it onto her lap, and slip out again before anyone was any the wiser.

She walked to the stairs and down to the lobby as quickly as she could without attracting attention.

It was only when she was crossing the lobby towards the front entrance that she realised she was gripping the key to Miz Walsh's room as if her fingers were paralysed round it.

She stopped on the spot, swore at herself for her stupidity and stood for a moment, indecisive, between the urge to flee and the urge to do the right thing.

While she was standing there a man in a suit, like the others now in the Hall, went past her, looking her up and down as if assessing a pile of goods in a shop, and that decided her.

She turned, walked to the lift with a new determination, rose to the fifth floor, and entered room five-four-five again.

Having acted on the impulse of the moment, now she was in the room, her nerve failed her. And suddenly she felt hungry.

She sat in the armchair and gobbled up the slices of toast and drank the remains of the orange juice as if she hadn't eaten in days. It was comforting and made her feel better at once.

She was beginning to relax when there was a knock at the door.

She sat still while her heart raced. Surely it couldn't be the author? She'd be giving her talk by now. And anyway, why would she knock?

The knocking again, followed this time by a man's voice, 'Room service.'

Ursula kept still, more from fright than intention.

Then she heard a key being inserted and the door opened.

A young man in hotel uniform — maroon waistcoat, white shirt, black tie, black trousers — came in, saw her, stopped short and said, 'Oh, sorry, miss! No one answered. I've come for the breakfast tray.'

Ursula was still too shocked to say anything. The young man took the tray, turned at the door, looked at her, said, 'Sorry to disturb you,' and left.

The intrusion had panicked her. But now a thought came to her and with it a renewed determination.

She undressed, flinging her clothes — Imogen's clothes — onto the bed, followed by her bra and panties, and went into the bathroom, where she turned on the shower, used the loo while the water was hotting up, then got into the cubicle and with a sense of release so pleasurable she laughed out loud, shampooed her hair from the little bottle provided, soaped herself vigorously with the little bar of soap provided, rubbed herself hard all over with the face cloth provided, then stood, face up, eyes closed under the showerhead, while the refreshing water sluiced away the shampoo and the soap, and with them the hair spray and makeup the department store specialist had taken so long to apply, and which since the moment she had left the store had oppressed her with a sense of fraudulence and caused her to be treated as someone she was not and knew now she did not wish to be.

When she got out of the shower, she looked at herself in the full-length mirror on the door of the wardrobe opposite the bathroom. It was such a relief to be clean, to be free of clothes, to be only herself, her own flesh and bones.

Why is it, she asked herself, that I feel better with nothing on? Why do I prefer to be naked than in clothes? I think I'd like to be naked all the time!

She regarded herself, that way and this, up and down.

I'm sure I look better naked, she told herself. And I feel whole.

That's it! she thought. When I'm naked I feel whole. I never feel right in clothes. Whatever I wear feels wrong. I can never find anything that looks right everywhere on me. Clothes seem to separate my top half from my bottom half, my head from my body. Without anything on I'm all one.

V

A quarter of an hour later, Ursula was sitting in the armchair, dressed only in a luxurious bathrobe with the hotel's name blazoned on the chest, which she had found hanging on the back of the bathroom door. She was reading Griselda Walsh's new book while she cooled off and her hair dried.

She calculated that Miz Walsh would be gone to at least twelve thirty and probably not return to her room till after the conference lunch, at which she would be a guest of honour, wouldn't she? Plenty of time before she needed to dress, hand in the key at reception, pretending she had found it on the floor, and leave without being discovered.

Miz Walsh had treated her as Cindy. Using the author's room to turn Cindy into Ursula wasn't exactly what Miz Walsh had intended. But Cindy decided it was a gift anyway.

But she was only a few pages into the book when there was a knock on the door again, and the same voice saying, 'Room service.'

This time, she wasn't so panicked.

'What do you want?' she called back.

'It's room service, miss,' the man said. 'I need to speak to you.'

'What about?'

'Private, miss.'

Fearing he'd go on shouting and draw the attention of other guests or staff, she opened the door enough to see him. He wasn't in hotel uniform but just his white shirt and a pair of old jeans, and a large canvas bag hanging from his shoulder. And he wasn't really a man either, but a boy not much older than herself.

'What do you want?' Ursula said, trying to be authoritative but her nerves sounding in her voice.

'This isn't your room, is it?' the boy said. 'It's the author's, Griselda Walsh's. I know because I brought her breakfast this morning.'

Ursula stared at him.

The boy waited a moment before saying, 'Have you permission to be here?'

'She sent me to get something for her,' Ursula said.

'So why are you in a bathrobe?'

Ursula was stuck.

'I'll have to report you to security,' the boy said. 'Because if they find out I knew you were here when you shouldn't be, I'll get the sack, and I can't afford to lose this job. We're supposed to report anything unusual. You might be a thief . . . or a terrorist.'

'Don't be so ridiculous,' Ursula heard herself say.

'You'd be surprised what goes on in hotels,' the boy said. 'So what are you doing here?'

Ursula opened the door wide and said, 'Nothing. Just . . . nothing.'

The boy laughed. 'So I tell security there's a girl in room five-four-five who's doing nothing, do I?'

'I mean I'm not doing anything wrong.'

'Except using someone's room without permission.'

Ursula felt close to tears.

'I was just . . . I don't know . . . having a day out.'

'A day out?'

'Yes.'

'You'll have to come up with something better than that.'

'Look . . . I came to the hotel to try and see Griselda Walsh because I like her books, and she found me and thought I was one of the staff or something and asked me to get a jacket from her room because she was feeling cold and she went into the meeting and I came and got her jacket and gave it to her but forgot to give her the key and I was feeling a bit, well, annoyed, because I'd had a makeup makeover and been whistled at in the street and made a pass at by a man in Costa Coffee and I felt upset at being treated like I was a, well, like something I'm not, and when I found I still had the key I came up and had a shower to wash off all the makeup and stuff and was cooling down afterwards and I was going to hand in the key when I left but you came for the tray and now you've come back accusing me of being a thief or a terrorist and I know I shouldn't have done it, but that's why.'

The boy gave her a wary look.

'Please don't report me,' Ursula said. 'I'm harmless, really I am!'

'All right,' he said. 'But I think I'd better make sure you leave without taking anything and the place is tidy. Then I'll see you out of the hotel and that way everything should be all right.'

Ursula let him in, and closed the door.

They stood at the foot of the bed looking at each other.

'I can't go till I get dressed,' Ursula said. 'I'll use the bathroom, OK?'

The boy nodded.

Ursula collected her things and went into the bathroom. She was trembling all the time she was dressing.

When she came out, the boy was sitting in the armchair, his bag on his knees.

'You're not in uniform,' she said.

'Finished my shift at twelve.'

Ursula sat on the bed and pulled on her shoes.

'What's your name?' the boy asked.

'Ursula Oracod. What's yours?'

'Paul. Paul Taylor.'

'Hi.'

'Hi.'

'Look,' Ursula said. 'I'm sorry. I've been stupid, I know.'

'It's OK. No problem. It's just, I mustn't lose this job. I need the money.'

'I'll tidy the bathroom, make sure it's as I found it.'

'No, I'll do it. I know how things are supposed to be.'

He got up and went to the bathroom.

'Done,' he said, coming back.

Ursula stood up. Paul looked round the room, squared off the bed cover, checked the bedside tables, and adjusted the vase of flowers on the coffee table.

'What about the key?' Ursula said. 'I was going to hand it in at reception and say I'd found it.'

'That's a bit risky. Reception might ask for your details. I'll hand it in myself. Where did you take her jacket?'

'To the Princess Diana Hall. I met her outside there.'

'OK, that's where I'll say I found it. I'll take you down, see you out, then hand in the key. OK?'

'OK. And look — thanks.'

'Yeah, well! I'll tell you something. I'm not too keen on Griselda Walsh. I brought her breakfast this morning and all I got was complaints. She wanted it at eight thirty. I was ten minutes late. I couldn't help it, room service is busy at that time. Then she rang down and complained the coffee wasn't hot, so I had to rush up with another pot. When I got here she nagged on about the toast being cold, which has nothing to do with me, I just carry the stuff. I told her that and she said I was being cheeky. Forward was the word she used. *Forward!* When I left she phoned reception and put in a complaint about the inefficiency of room service, gave them my name, and said I'd been rude to her.'

'How did she know who you were?'

'We wear name tags on our jackets. My boss gave me a telling off. So she really got up my nose. Some guests do. Whatever you do there's no pleasing them. They seem to think you're their personal servant and have nothing else to do but look after them.'

'Sounds as if you don't like your job much.'

'I don't.'

'So why do it?'

'I need the money to go to art school next year. And the hours suit me. I'm finished at twelve, and the rest of the day I can do my own work. I need to build up a portfolio of drawings and paintings to qualify.'

'You want to be an artist?'

He suddenly blushed, looked shy, put his head down, and said, 'We'd better go.'

VI

Outside, Ursula waited.

She hoped Paul would leave by the hotel's main entrance.

Which he did about ten minutes later.

She caught up with him as he walked down the street.

'Hey—you again!' he said, smiling, and stopping to face her.

'Hi,' Ursula said. 'Look, I'm sorry I did that. I mean, nearly got you into trouble.'

'No problem.'

'But I'd like to thank you. Could I buy you a coffee? Or maybe we could have something to eat?'

'One of the few good things about being on room service is there's always plenty to eat. You should see what people send back untouched.'

'OK. Just a thought. Thanks, anyway.'

She was turning to go when Paul said, 'Hang on a sec. It's a nice day. I've been inside since six this morning. I wouldn't mind a walk in the park. If that doesn't sound too corny.'

'Who cares if it is?'

They set off. The park was only a few minutes away.

'I come here quite a bit,' Paul said as they sauntered along the path through the trees towards the lake. 'I like looking at the people, and the ducks on the pond are always good for a laugh. I've done quite a few drawings here.'

'I like painting,' Ursula said. 'Or used to. But I was no good at it.'

'Did you draw?'

'No. Just paint.'

'You've got to draw if you want to paint well.'

'Why?'

'It trains your hand, and it makes you look very closely at what you're drawing. That's the main thing about art. Looking very closely. And for a long time.'

'I wish I could see some of your drawings.'

'You can. I've got some in my bag.'

They sat on a bench. Paul pulled a sketchpad out of his bag and opened it to show Ursula.

There were all sorts of sketches, some very quick, hardly more than a few lines, some more finished. There were some that were of small boxes arranged together, some of people sitting on park benches, some of children playing in the sand tray, a boy on a swing, a number of ducks on the water. And three of a nude woman sitting on a box.

Paul commentated as he showed Ursula each picture.

'I did the boxes after looking at some drawings by Morandi, who had a thing about boxes and bottles. Lovely drawings. Very still. Like drawings of silence. Very hard to do, though. Getting the arrangement right . . . I did these ones of the people in the park last week . . . I did the nudes in life class this week. I should do more life studies. It's important. And I need them for my portfolio.'

'So why don't you?'

'It costs too much. If you're not a student, you can attend life classes only if you pay. And I'm trying to save up for when I go to art school.'

Ursula looked at the drawings. They seemed very good to her. She wished she could draw as well.

'Can I do a drawing of you?' Paul asked.

'What, now, you mean?'

'Why not?'

'I've never been drawn before. What do I have to do?'

'Nothing. Just sit and watch the ducks. And we can go on talking. You can manage that?'

She smiled at him.

'I can manage that!'

'OK. Let's do it! Stay where you are.'

He propped himself against the arm of the bench, knees up, feet on the seat, took a pencil from his bag, propped his drawing pad on his knees, looked at Ursula sitting in profile at the other end of the bench, and started sketching.

For a while nothing was said. Paul worked at his drawing. Ursula watched the ducks. But all the time she was aware, even though she wasn't looking at him, that Paul was examining her closely. She felt as if his eyes were touching her, travelling over her face and body, feeling every curve and shape, muscle and bone. It was the strangest sensation she had ever felt. And it became so intense that she couldn't help speaking in order to release the tension building up inside her.

'Do you have brothers and sisters?' she asked.

'No. Only child. You?'

'Two sisters. One older, one younger.'

'That's nice.'

'Is it?'

'Isn't it? I'd quite like to have a sister. When I was little, I used to collect the tops off cornflake packets.'

'What?'

'The tops off cornflake packets. My mother said if I

collected enough of them I could exchange them for a sister.'

'She didn't!'

'It's true.'

Ursula couldn't help laughing.

'Sit still. And look serious again.'

'But cornflake packets! And you believed her!'

'Didn't you believe your mother when you were little?'

That put a silence on Ursula.

Paul said, 'I used to go round the neighbours asking for the tops off their cornflake packets, till my mother found out and said it only worked if they were the tops off packets of cornflakes I'd eaten. I gave up after I'd saved thirty-four and my mother said it still wasn't enough.'

'She was only trying to make you eat your cornflakes.'

'Oh, how cynical you are, Ursula Oracod!'

'Yeah, well, maybe I am.'

Paul worked on.

'Can I have a look?' Ursula said.

'No,' Paul said. 'It's not right yet. I'm going to start again.'

He flipped the page over.

'Could you turn a bit and face me three quarters on?'

Ursula shifted into a new pose. Now she could see him as he worked.

He started again, looking as closely as before. She felt he was x-raying her, seeing right through into her insides.

'What do your parents think of you wanting to be an artist?'

'They're separated. My mother is married to someone else and lives in Scotland. Don't see her much.'

'You live with your father?'

'When they split up I was given the choice. Bad decision!'

'Why?'

'I was ten when they split up. I liked him then. We did a lot together. Football matches. Fishing. Gardening—he's a big gardener, and very good at it. But then I got the drawing bug. He didn't mind at first. But when I got serious about it, he wasn't so keen. Then when I decided I wanted to go to art school and be a professional artist, he really turned.'

'Why?'

'He doesn't know anything about art. And doesn't much like what he does know. Thinks it's only for the rich and what he calls the phonies and the pseuds and people with their heads up their bums. Not a job for a man. And how many so-called artists make a living out of it anyway? Et cetera. We had a big row about it. You get the idea.'

'I do.'

'So the deal is, either I get what he calls a proper job, or he'll chuck me out.'

'And that's why you're working at the hotel?'

'And why I'm saving up. When I get into art school, *if* I get in, I'll have to find somewhere else to live and pay my own way.'

'I'm sorry.'

'Nar! Don't be. I don't mind. I did at first, after the row. It really upset me then. But not now. Somehow, I like it. I like knowing I'll have to do it all myself without any help from him.'

'Why?'

'Because that's the proof it really matters to me. That I really do want to study art and be an artist. It's only when you're on your own, no one, nothing to fall back on, and people are against it, that you know you're really meant to do what you want to do.'

Ursula thought for a few minutes. Paul went on with his drawing.

'Parents are odd,' Ursula said.

'Yours too?' Paul asked.

'You could say.'

'Why, what's so odd about them?'

Ursula couldn't reply at once. She'd touched the

unmentionable. The thing never talked about at home. The thing she'd never told anyone.

She looked at Paul, so absorbed in his drawing, looked at his eyes, which looked at her with an intensity that seemed to both see her and see through her. No one had ever looked at her like this before. And it was as if at that moment nothing else mattered to him except Ursula and the marks he was making on the paper that were her too as he had discovered her from the explorations of his eyes.

She felt excited and yet calm. It was as if he were seeking her out. Trying to understand her completely. It was thrilling.

His total attention seemed to draw from her like a magnet the truth she had never told anyone else.

'They're odd,' she said. 'They're odd, because I'm not . . . Well . . . You see, after my eldest sister was born, Imogen, my mother had an affair. It didn't last long. She says it was an infatuation. A fling . . . My dad . . . well, he isn't my dad . . . but he was very busy, away a lot for his job . . . Anyway, my mother had this fling with another man. But she got pregnant with me. She told my dad . . . I mean not my dad but . . . she told him, and he went ape. But somehow they patched it up and he said he'd accept me as his so long as no one ever knew . . . And they kept the secret till I was thirteen, when Imogen overheard an argument they were having . . . They thought no one was in the house but Imogen was and heard them . . . And my father who isn't my father reminded my mother about her fling and me . . . Afterwards Imogen tackled them about it. And so my mother told me because she knew Imogen would if she didn't, because Imogen is like that. After that both my sisters . . . my half sisters . . . never liked me. They said I wasn't really their sister anymore, and . . . Well, that's it. That's why my parents are odd.'

Paul had stopped drawing while Ursula was talking. He looked at her now, not as a model but as the girl who was sitting with him on a park bench and had begun to cry.

'I'm sorry,' he said.

'Don't be!' Ursula said with the same tone of voice as Paul had used to her, and looking at him through water-eyes, smiled, and added, 'I don't mind. I did at first. But not now.'

Paul smiled back at her echoing his words.

'At least they haven't threatened to chuck me out,' she added.

'Maybe,' Paul said, 'we could both do with something to drink?'

Ursula nodded and wiped the tears away.

Paul handed her a paper hankie. 'I use them for making smudges on my drawings,' he said.

'More to being an artist than meets the eye,' Ursula said.

'More to being most people than meets the eye,' Paul said.

'That's for sure,' Ursula said.

They walked across the park to a café by the gate, bought a couple of cans of Coke and sat at a picnic table outside.

Ursula had recovered herself. Paul had gone quiet.

'Can I see your drawing?' Ursula asked.

Paul took his pad from his bag, opened it, and put it down on the table in front of her.

She was looking at herself as she had never seen herself before, and yet it was *herself* as she felt inside.

She was so surprised she couldn't say anything.

'You don't like it,' Paul said.

'I love it.' Ursula could only just get the words out. Tears were forming again.

'You do?'

She looked at him, eye to eye.

'I don't know what to say.'

'You're saying it,' he said.

He reached over, touched her cheek with a finger, and drew it down to her chin.

'Some people have beautiful faces,' he said. 'Or you think so when you first see them. But when you draw them, when you look really close, you find there's nothing much in them—nothing much *behind* them, if you know what I mean? And some people who you don't think are beautiful at first, when you draw them, you see they are, because of what's *behind* them—what's *in* them. And they are the faces that are really beautiful. Your face is like that.'

Ursula drank the last of her Coke and squeezed the tin till it crumpled.

They regarded each other. There was a new understanding between them.

'You know something?' Ursula said.

'What?'

'When I was in the hotel room I had a shower and afterwards I looked at myself in the mirror. And you know what?'

'What?'

'I realised I don't like clothes. I never feel right in them. I never seem to be me in them. But without clothes I feel whole. I feel *myself*.'

Paul smiled.

'Do you understand what I mean?' Ursula said.

'Sure I do. And do you know what?'

'What?'

'You looked a lot better after your shower than you did before.'

'How do you know?'

'Because I saw you dressed when I collected the tray and I saw you after you'd showered.'

'When I was in a bathrobe.'

'True. But you still looked better.'

'You really think so?'

'I do.'

Ursula waited a moment, to be sure she wanted to say what now came into her head.

'You know you said you needed to do more . . . what did you call them . . . life studies?'

'Drawings of nudes.'

'And how they are expensive and you can't afford them?'

'Are you going where I think you're going?'

Ursula gave him a wry smile. 'Maybe!'

'Would you?'

'I'd like to, if you would.'

'If I would what?'

'Like to draw me naked.'

He laughed. 'Would I!'

'Then let's do it.'

'You're sure?'

Ursula nodded.

'With one condition,' she said.

'Which is?'

'You're naked too!'

Paul roared and drummed a tattoo on the table with his hands.

'Why should men have all the fun?' Ursula said.

'OK,' Paul said. 'It's a deal.'

Now Ursula was bubbling with laughter.

'No, no! I was only joking!'

'But you're right. And you know what they say about jokes?'

'No, what do they say?'

'Jokes always tell the truth. So that's what you want! And that's how it will be. Both of us starkers!'

When they had got over their laughter, Ursula said, 'Where and when?'

'My house, tomorrow afternoon. My dad will be at work, not back till six. So we'll be OK.'

'What about I wait for you outside the hotel at twelve and you can take me home with you?'

'Good thinking.'

So it was arranged. And Ursula hadn't felt so happy since before the unmentionable was revealed.

On the way home she passed the library, but felt too excited to go in and speak to Martin. I'll see him tomorrow before meeting Paul, she decided. I'll tell him that I met Griselda Walsh and I've started her new book but already feel I've grown out of her books now. I won't tell him that they are Cindy's books, not

Ursula Oracod's. And Cindy doesn't exist anymore. She never really did. Just like the stories in Griselda Walsh's books. They aren't real. They're only fantasies. Cindy liked fantasies. They comforted her. Ursula Oracod likes real life.

When she arrived home everyone was out.

She changed into her own clothes, put Imogen's back where she'd found them and sat in her room imagining tomorrow afternoon.

Imogen and Beatrice turned up an hour later. They were banging on, as usual, about their day's excitements.

Imogen had chucked her latest boyfriend.

Beatrice had bought a new pair of shoes.

They were planning an evening of boy hunting.

'Oh, hey, Cindy,' Imogen said, 'what's for supper? Could you rustle up a pizza for us? We need to change and get going.'

'No,' Ursula said. 'I couldn't. If you want any rustling done, why not do it yourselves for a change? And by the way, my name is Ursula, not Cindy. And that goes from now on. OK?'

She left them to their shocked stares, returned to her room, and managed to retain her victory smile until she had closed her door.

The Scientific Approach

MY GIRLFRIEND HAS A NEW BOYFRIEND NOW.

The athletic type.

Not as tall as me. I look down at him.

He doesn't look at me.

Beside him I feel weedy.

He has black hair, cut very short all over, bristly.

Needs to shave every day already so doesn't, just to prove he could.

Wouldn't have thought he'd be her type.

Maybe it was me who wasn't but she didn't know till she tried.

Like with her clothes. She'd put something on, certain it was what she wanted, then decide it wasn't, put something else on that was quite different, and say it was exactly right.

Trial and error.

Nothing wrong with that.

The scientific approach.

She'd do the same with food.

We'd go somewhere — Mac's, Papa's Pizzas, KFC, wherever — buy what we wanted.

She'd take a bite or two of hers and then say she wished she'd chosen something else. I'd say 'What?' she'd say, 'What you've got,' and I'd say, 'Have mine, and I'll have yours.'

We'd swap and she'd be happy.

Got to the point where I'd always buy what I thought she'd like and suggest to her that she buy something I'd like. Very offhand, not, you know, *assertive*, or she wouldn't do it. I wouldn't say I'd like it, you understand, only suggest she might. She'd buy that, take a bite or two, say, 'I wish I'd chosen something else,' I'd say, 'Have mine,' and that would be that, both of us happy.

She never blamed me for suggesting she choose what she chose and then not wanting it. She's not like that at all, never tries to put the blame on the other person. She's good that way.

Never blames herself either.

Just gets on with it because that's the way life is.

I was sitting in the Happy Eater.

Don't like the Happy Eater much. Don't like it at all, to tell the truth. But my girlfriend's new boyfriend does. I've often seen him going in there.

They came in. She saw me. Waved. Smiled. No animosity between us. Didn't ever split up really. Not the way some do. *Acrimoniously*, if you know what I mean. She just said she wanted to go out with her new boyfriend, did I mind? I said she should do what she wanted, it was her choice. I knew she would anyway. Saying I minded wouldn't have stopped her.

She did and we haven't been out together since.

She brought him over to where I was sitting, at a table for four, no one else there. She sat opposite, he sat beside her.

They'd been to a football match, she said.

Not my sort of thing.

She was all fresh air and rosy cheeks.

Very my sort of thing.

Going on to a party at one of his mates. Birthday party, parents leaving them to it. Be a smash. She said he wanted to eat before they went. 'Get stoked up' is how she put it. Not her sort of talk usually.

He said nothing, just ate. French fries, pie, French fries. Lots of fries. Lovely manners. Chewed with his mouth open. Breathed through his mouth at the same time. You know what I mean.

Didn't look at me once.

She asked why I was at the Happy Eater, knowing I didn't like it. Said I felt like a change.

She asked what I was doing after. Said I was going to a movie.

Wasn't, just said it. She always liked going to movies. Just about her favourite thing. Holding hands. Always held hands. She liked holding hands, said it was the best part. Didn't matter whether the film was good or bad, what she liked was being in the dark, the warmth, being close together, and holding hands while watching the movie.

I like holding hands as well.

She also liked ice cream before the start. ('Wish I'd chosen yours.' 'Swap.')

She asked if I was going with anyone. I said no.

She wanted to know which movie. Said I'd make up my mind when I got there.

She didn't say anything after that.

Gave him a long look though.

He said nothing, except, 'Don't you want that?' meaning her food, which she'd only taken a bite or two of. She said, 'No, I wish I'd chosen something else.' He said, 'I'll have it, then,' and took it and ate it, head down, using his fork like a shovel, mouth open, breathing.

His hair really is very short. Not like mine, which is longish and thick. 'Nice,' she used to say, running her fingers through it. Could see his scalp through the bristles. Grey. I'd thought it would be nicely tanned like the rest of him, but it wasn't, it was grey. Like the skin of a lizard. Put me off my food, to be honest.

When he finished, he got up straightaway and they left.

She looked back at me from the door, and smiled.

When I thought it was about right, I walked to the cinema.

Stood in the foyer.

Studied what was showing on each of the five screens. Picked out the one I wanted to see and the one I'd suggest.

Don't think she fancies boys any more than I do.

Kangaroo

I SHOULDN'T HAVE TAKEN THE JOB.

I wouldn't have, if I'd known I would be a kangaroo.

All it said in the advert was *Want to be an animal and be paid for it? If you do, your local theme park needs you.*

I applied. Met the 'human resources manager'—a middle-aged woman in a black pin-striped suit pretending to be a man.

I'd have turned tail there and then but needed the money.

You know what it's like in the summer. Or it is for me, anyway. The word 'holiday' does not exist in my father's vocabulary. I am expected to 'apply' myself, as he puts it, 'find out how the world works', 'engage in gainful employment', and generally 'improve my knowledge of people and life'. Otherwise, no more weekly allowance.

I wouldn't say my father is mean or harsh. Strict, yes. Careful with money, yes. Canny, my grandfather calls it (with a wink and usually when bunging me an extra dole of cash). But not mean. He'll buy me pretty well anything, if he can afford it and thinks I deserve it, or it will 'assist your progress in life'. (The high quotient of pomposity in his diction is the result of too many overtime hours spent as a lowly clerk in a law firm; I think he thinks it makes him sound authoritative and wise.)

So the point is I needed a summer job, and there was nothing else on offer which I would demean myself by doing. I'm rubbish at waitressing—can't remember who ordered what and won't suffer imperious customers gladly. Refuse to be a barmaid and put up with the lewd jokes, gropes, passes, and inebriated slobberings of male boozers. And trying to sell anything is a humiliating experience, besides which I wouldn't give away the crap you're expected to persuade people to buy, never mind sell it. That left being an animal in the local theme park, which seemed like a reasonable solution to an otherwise intractable problem. As a little girl I'd had fun times there, those being days when my father still had some fun in him.

Because of what happened in the end, I'll have to tell you about my boyfriend, Bret, and my dad. They get on well together, which is one of the wonders of the world. For starters, Bret is the opposite of pompous. He's a bricklayer, which my father would usually think makes him not good enough for me. My dad is small and weedy and also very possessive of me, and more than a touch jealous. Bret is tall and well-built and thinks the world of me. And so, as I say, I can't imagine why they like each other, but they do. It's true they do have one thing in common. They are obsessed by the movies of Clint Eastwood. They watch them together all the time. They must know them backwards. 'Make my day' is a running joke between them.

Why my father likes such violent films is a puzzle I have yet to solve. My mother says it's his way of releasing pent-up aggression that boils up inside him, working as a humble office clerk. She also says he likes Bret because Bret is the kind of hunky male my dad wishes he was. And that he approves of Bret and me being together because he wants me to have that kind of man. (My dad as Bret, or Bret as my dad? I'd rather not think of that, thank you.)

Well, my mum could be right, she usually is. But I don't know. What I do know is that Bret turns me on, is always good to me, makes me laugh a lot, and I always feel safe when I'm with him. He's also five years older than me and is a proper man, not a silly boy, which is what all the boys my own age seem to be. What more could a girl want?

As for Bret, he says he likes my dad because my dad likes him, which I suppose is a good enough reason for liking someone.

Anyway, the point is I had to be an animal at the theme park as a summer job. Bret also approved, because he thought it was unlikely that, with me dressed as a stuffed animal, any rival predatory male would make a pass at me. As you'll guess from this, Bret is even more jealous of me than my dad is. The only time he gets really bad tempered is if another man comes on to me. I am secretly pleased by this, but of course, never let on to him that I am.

When I applied for the job I didn't know I'd be a kangaroo or I might have had second thoughts. Not that I have anything against kangaroos per se. I've only ever seen them in the flesh once, in a zoo. I don't exactly *like* them. They look like dusty creatures, and smelly, to me, and I don't like their little sharp faces and little forelegs that make a funny contrast with their big fat thighs and long back legs and long thick tails.

If I'd had any choice in the matter I'd have been a happy lion or a cuddly bear. But no go. The man called 'the coach' dished out the animals as soon as we turned up for the first session of the required two days of training, and as I was inevitably last to arrive, being always late however hard I try not to be, I was lumbered with being a kangaroo.

I should mention that 'the coach' was an Australian, and indicated as he handed me my costume that he regarded being a kangaroo an honour, it being a creature accorded special affection by his fellow Australians, for whom it was (is) a national symbol. Or is that a wallaby? I get them mixed up. (I'm rubbish at biology, names of animals, plants, trees, etc.) All I can say is there's no accounting for taste. I should also add that you did not argue with him, for the simple reason that he not only resembled but behaved like a sergeant major as seen in the American war movies my father enjoys—e.g., *Platoon*, *Apocalypse Now*, etc., etc. (if you haven't seen them, be thankful).

Not that I was the only kangaroo. There were three of us. There had to be three because it was so hot inside the costumes that health and safety regulations stipulated that no one was allowed to be in their animal costume for more than twenty minutes an hour in case you expired from overheating, hyperthermia, dehydration, and other forms of exhaustion. Which meant that three people were needed per animal, each with our own costume, so that there was always one of us on duty, 'performing' among the public while the other two rested. Twenty minutes on, forty minutes off, from opening time to closing time each day.

When I first heard this I thought the job was going to be a cinch. It was only when we did it that I realised how far from being an easy ride it was. I had to be out there kangarooing eight times a day, no letup, because I had to eat and drink a lot and use the loo and wash the sweat off (I needed two or three changes of underwear every day) and generally get my strength back during my forty minutes' 'rest'.

If you don't believe how difficult it is, try this. Dress yourself in three pairs of long johns and a winter puffer jacket with two blankets wrapped tightly round you, and then run about in the garden for twenty minutes on a hot day, and do it a few times with the required forty minutes off after every twenty, and then tell me if it isn't a version of torture.

But that wasn't all there was to it.

I had to hop like a kangaroo. I was 'coached' in this by the Ozzy sergeant major all of the first of the two days of 'training'; in the morning without the costume, in the afternoon with it on, which is when I began to suspect all would not be as fine and dandy as I had at first supposed. Hopping puts great strain on your leg muscles, especially those you don't usually employ in everyday human life. I was in need of physiotherapy after an hour of 'training'. I doubt I need report that none was on offer, the sergeant major's only comment when I complained being that I'd soon get used to it, no pain without gain ha-ha-ha.

Apart from hopping, I also had to learn a basic

sign language. Why? Because there was a strict rule, enforced by dismissal from the job if you broke it. The rule was: on no account must you ever speak to anyone while performing in public. You could not even make noises appropriate to your animal. Why? Because attention of the paying customers, *and especially the children*, must not be drawn to the fact that a human being is inside the animal costume. It would spoil the illusion, explained the aforementioned pin-striped human resources manager.

This would have seemed like a load of kangaroo dollop but for one fact. I remembered visiting this very theme park when I was little and being greeted by a cuddly animal as big as my dad and not only *believing* it, but *loving* it. And thinking back, I remembered that the animals never made a sound, but did wave their animal limbs about in ways that made perfect sense to me and did not seem in the slightest ridiculous. Rather, I suppose, like babies seem to understand baby-babble when to me now it is just a lot of twaddle. (Am I suited to motherhood? Perhaps not. It is a moot question yet to be addressed. Though on kangaroo evidence, probably not.)

Which is why the morning of the second day was spent practising how to say in your animal's sign language such simple messages as 'Hello!' 'Welcome to our wonderful park,' 'I'm so happy to see you,'

'No thank you' (for use when offered already licked ice creams, half-chewed sweets, bits of squashy fruit, weary sandwiches, and—as I soon learned when on the job—such an astonishing variety of other similar gifts as boggles the mind, including now and then a besotted little child's favourite toy, all of the aforelisted offered in tribute to your animal attraction). Finally there was 'Good-bye,' and if in dire need 'I have to go to sleep now'—necessary in order to extract yourself from difficult situations, as when a child hangs on to you, won't let go, and is about to explode into hysterics because you won't go home with him/her.

There was no sign language for such requests as 'Let go, you nasty little creep,' or for use with parents, 'Why don't you take your hideous offspring and bog off?' One of our major occupations during 'rest' periods was recounting to our fellow resting animals the most hilarious events and the worst of the horrors encountered during our previous twenty minutes on the job. If it hadn't been for this outlet I think we would all have gone bananas before the third day's work was over. (Except the chimpanzee animals, who of course pretended to eat bananas all the time, and were therefore already bananas. [Sorry! Bad joke.])

Not only did we have to keep silent, and in my case hop about 'in character', we also had to distribute leaflets to as many of the paying customers and their progeny as possible. The leaflets advertised events—such as rides on the big roller coaster, trips through the tunnel of love and on the ghost train, and the major screamer called the Drop Tower. In other words, the gallimaufry of enticements usually on offer in these places of fun and games, all of which cost extra. Needless to point out, our main job wasn't really entertaining the 'guests' (as pin-striped management insisted on calling them) but was advertising those 'attractions' that made the most money for the owners.

Because I was an animal of the marsupial variety, I had a pocket over my padded stomach, out of which poked the head of a 'baby roo', and in which I soon found it convenient to keep my stock of leaflets, one of which I would pull from my marsupial pouch with a grand gesture of generosity when saying good-bye to a juvenile 'guest' after going through my ritual of 'Hello. Lovely to see you. How wonderful you look. And now here's a nice gift for you . . .' Leaflet produced as from a conjuror's magic hat and presented as if a gift from the gods.

Though I say it myself, I very quickly became rather good at this performance, and though I do say it myself I wasn't the only one to say it. So did our 'coach', the aforementioned Ozzy sergeant major, who barked out at me as I came in for my required forty-minute rest on the second afternoon of work, 'Now then, girl, I can tell you a real live roo couldn't do a better job with those leaflets than you do.' I was aware that this was praise indeed, which encouraged me to develop my 'act' all the more. (How easily we are seduced by praise into doing that which, without it, we would despise and abandon.)

Not that praise alone was the only spur. More true to say it was the fact that we were assessed by how many 'guests' we 'welcomed' and how many leaflets we got rid of during each twenty-minute shift. If we dispensed above a certain number we notched up a 'star' (!infant school here we come!), which in turn, if sufficient stars were collected, qualified you for a bonus at the end of the week. (By the way, despite valiant efforts from one and all, not least yours truly, I never heard of anyone actually achieving such reward. It took us two weeks to realise that the target was set so high, you'd have to be super animal to reach it.)

Well, dear friends, I have to report that pride does indeed cometh before a fall, as the wise old saying warns.

And in my case it cometh about in this wise.

The Tuesday of my third week as a kangaroo. Very hot. Big crowds. Busy busy busy.

Afternoon. My sixth stint of the day. My twenty minutes were up. I knew because there was a big clock on the wall above the door to the offices and the room where we rested. No sign of Laura, the girl who was meant to take over from me. So I kept going, expecting her to turn up at any minute. But the minutes went by and she didn't. (Learned later she had been sick. The heat had got to her, and she was too weak to come out. The other girl, who could have stood in for her, had gone for a sandwich.)

I was sweating pretty heavily by the time I'd done thirty minutes, and was feeling cross with Laura, which didn't help. I'd done very well during my allotted time. So well that I ran out of leaflets. Gave the last one to a little girl who had followed me around but had been too shy to come up to me.

As I handed her my last leaflet, I thought, OK, that's it, I'm going in whether Laura comes out or not.

I gave the little girl the leaflet and did my sign language stuff on the lines of 'Isn't that terrific! What a pretty girl you are! Good-bye, I'm going now.' At which moment a large boy, who had been watching me for most of my stint, started taking the mickey by exaggeratedly copying my movements.

I tried to ignore him. Turned to start my kangaroo hopping to the office door. But he blocked the way.

I stopped and gave him the usual 'Hello. Lovely to

see you' routine. But he just stood there and glared. He was almost as tall as me and far too old to be cuddling up with a stuffed kangaroo. Mostly, the older kids didn't bother with us, or just stood by and watched with a knowing smile as their much younger brothers and sisters enjoyed themselves.

But this boy was trouble. That was obvious from the glassy look in his eyes.

'Give us me leaflet,' he said in a voice that made it clear he wasn't playing.

I did my 'Oh, look! None left!' routine, which I'd used before when I'd run out. 'I'll go and get you one. Wait here!'

The boy didn't move.

'Give us me leaflet and give us it *now*,' he said in tones as unyielding as granite. 'You've given everybody else one. I want mine.' Quite clearly a major thug in the making.

'Sorry,' I signed. 'None left. Now I must go to sleep.'

'Give us me leaflet,' the boy said, 'or it's the casualty ward for you.'

'I have to go now,' I signed, and started to hop round him.

But he dodged sideways, never taking his glassy eyes off me, and blocked my way again. This way and that. Whichever way I tried to go.

A crowd had gathered by now. From the look on

their faces, it was clear they supposed this was all part of the entertainment.

'Box his ears!' a man shouted.

'Yeah!' another added. 'Let's see you give him the kangaroo kick.'

After the fourth or fifth—I forget which—attempt to get past him, I'd had enough. Sweat was pouring off me, I thought I'd faint inside my costume before long, so I gave up, stood four square on my kangaroo legs and in plain human-being language said, 'Get out of the way, please.'

'Yar! See!' the boy shouted, addressing the assembled throng. 'See, it isn't a kangaroo at all.'

The crowd, or at least the adults and older kids, laughed. This was of course not news to them but, as I have learned is the case with people, they just loved the pretence being broken, the actuality revealed, the play-acting undone.

The little girl I'd given the last leaflet to, who was still watching, said something to her mother, who replied, at which the little girl burst into tears, broke free of her mother, ran up to me, threw the leaflet on the ground at my feet, and ran back to her mother, who she grabbed round the legs, hiding her face, crying profusely.

No doubt the truth had been revealed and had not been well received.

'Now look what you've done!' the boy shouted. 'You're a phony, that's what you are. You're not a kangaroo. You're just a dressed-up idiot.'

By now he was quite clearly enjoying himself and the attention he was receiving, not to mention the encouragement from the assembled throng.

'Push off, you nasty little creep!' I said to him.

'What did you call me?' he shouted. 'She called me a nasty little creep,' he yelled at the crowd.

The crowd hissed and booed.

'Go home, you little thug!'

'*What! Did you hear? She called me a little thug. Well, that's it!*'

And he launched a no-holds-barred attack, punching and kicking and generally giving a convincing impression of a determination to keep his promise to consign me to hospital.

As my costume was well padded, especially round the middle, and my legs were also padded to make the shape of a kangaroo's big thighs, his punches and kicks were cushioned. But they were still strong enough to knock me back.

I tried to hold him off, but I was half-hearted and he was full-hearted. I was only trying to keep him off me. He was on a mission to reduce me to a pile of— let's say effluent, rather than the words he was yelling at me.

I stumbled backwards a few steps. But a stuffed kangaroo costume is not designed either for full frontal attack, nor for retreating. My tail got tangled with my kangaroo legs, tied them up and prevented me taking any more steps, while the boy's battering pushed my top half backwards.

The inevitable result was that I tumbled to the ground.

This was not sufficient to satisfy the boy. He piled on top of me, belabouring me with a rain of blows that my costume—which was thin at the shoulders and on the head—did little to protect me from.

By now I was screaming a string of epithets I'd rather not record here. I used words I didn't know I knew.

Then the last straw, he got hold of my kangaroo head and pulled it off, revealing my screaming head to view.

The crowd gasped.

'There! Ya see!' the boy yelled. 'It's just a stupid girl!'

Heaven knows what would have happened if at that moment the boy hadn't been hauled off me by two burly security guards.

At the same time two of their colleagues lifted me to my feet and frog-marched me into the office.

There I was undressed, first aid applied to my

bruised face and body, water offered and consumed. It was only then I realised what had happened, the shock of which caused me to tremble so badly I couldn't hold anything or move for at least fifteen minutes.

Apparently, some people in the crowd had at last understood that the spectacle they were finding so amusing was not part of the official entertainment but was a real act of assault and someone had run to get help.

And the result?

The boy was given a telling off by one of the 'security personnel' and accompanied to the entrance of the theme park and told to go home or charges of assault would be laid against him. Apparently his response to this was to tell the security personnel to go and have sexual intercourse with themselves, before he ran off laughing.

I was given the sack.

Reasons enumerated by the pin-striped 'human resources manager':

1. I had broken the twenty-minute rule.
2. I had committed the unpardonable sin of speaking to a 'guest'.
3. I had used 'inappropriate language'.
4. My 'child management skills' had been shown to be wanting.

No explanation or reason was accepted.

'I'm afraid we cannot turn a blind eye to such behaviour or other members of staff might break the rules also, thinking them immune from reprimand. I do understand you were provoked and the boy behaved disgracefully. But we are a business and our reputation for responsible behaviour and the safety of our guests *whatever the provocation* are of the highest priority. So I'm afraid we'll have to let you go, despite your otherwise exemplary record.'

I was paid the full week's wage, though I had worked only two days of the week, and asked not to return to the park, even as a 'guest', for at least a year.

But that wasn't the end of it.

I was with Bret a few nights after I was let go — or, to use the proper word, sacked. We were walking from the movies when I saw the boy who attacked me hanging about on the other side of the street, and pointed him out to Bret, just as a matter of interest.

Before you could say 'Clint Eastwood', Bret strode across the road, grabbed the boy by the ear, and hauled him back to me, the boy stumbling and squawking fit to give you a headache. Not that I was silent myself. As soon as I realised what Bret was up to, I shouted, 'No, Bret, leave it!' But neither the boy's squealing nor my pleading had the slightest effect.

When they reached me, Bret flicked the boy's feet from under him so that he fell onto his knees in front of me, like a sinner confessing his sins. Only he didn't confess, he started swearing and cursing. Honestly, the words that boy knew! There were some I didn't even know myself.

'Shut it, punk,' Bret said.

The boy didn't.

Bret bent down and said something into the boy's ear.

This had an instant effect. The boy shut up.

(Afterwards, I asked Bret what he'd said. He replied, 'Man stuff. Don't ask.')

Then he said to the boy, 'I'll give you a choice, punk. You can apologise to my girl for what you did to her.'

'Or what?' said the boy, giving Bret a defiant look.

'Or you can make my day,' Bret said, with a broad grin.

Would you believe it! I mean, honestly! It was all I could do to keep a straight face. But I knew better than to laugh. I don't think men have much of a sense of humour when they go on like that.

I managed to say seriously and very firmly, 'Leave it, Bret, please. It won't mean anything even if he does.'

'You sure?' Bret said.

'He'd only lie, just to get away.'

'You hear that, punk?' Bret said. 'You hear what my

girl says? You should thank her as well as apologise. But let me make myself clear. If you ever come near her again, I will make it my business, and it will be my pleasure, to seriously rearrange the contours of your face. Comprendy, punk? Now scat!'

Which, after only a brief check of Bret's face to make sure, is what the boy did, with scrambling speed.

When I told what happened to my friend Sharon, who is mad about biology and so clever it makes you sick, she said with a knowing smile, 'A perfect example of mate guarding.'

I didn't need to Google 'mate guarding' to know what she meant.

Sharon says it's a mistake to forget that we human beings are animals first and whatever else second. But whether evolution will ever screen out from our animal nature the drive that causes a boy to attack a girl pretending to be a kangaroo, or the drive that causes a male to guard his mate just as violently, who knows?

All I know is I will never pretend to be a kangaroo again, or any other kind of animal, come to that.

The animal I am is quite enough to be going on with, thank you.

As for my Bret and what he did that day. Men! What more can I say.

Expulsion

Mr. Pearson, Sir,

You instructed me to write a letter of apology for not attending compulsory sport every Wednesday afternoon for the past six weeks. You also instructed me to explain in detail what I did with the time. You said that if I did not explain you would recommend my expulsion from school.

I'd better say straight off, Sir, that I cannot apologise.

I know sports afternoons are compulsory, but that does not mean doing the sports you, Sir, approve of and organise.

I have inquired about this with my form tutor, the Deputy Head of School, and the Head of Sixth Form. (I did not say why I was asking, or tell them about your threat. I simply put the question as a matter of general interest.) They each agreed that the purpose of sports afternoon is to ensure we take exercise. In other words, it isn't about *the sport* itself, but about *our health*. They agreed that exercise can be taken in many ways, not only by playing football, which is your personal sporting preference. I admit it is my least favourite of all sports.

I enjoy walking, climbing trees, and tennis in season. (As a matter of fact, I prefer sex to all of these, which I have read is as good exercise as any sport.) None of these (least of all sex) is laid on by you during compulsory sport. So I exercise myself in those ways at other times in the week, like after school and at weekends.

According to the advice given in the government document *Health and Exercise for School Children*, DfES C5 66/B, p. 14 (available, Sir, on the government's website, if you happen to have missed it), the recommended average for people of my age is a minimum of three hours of 'strenuous activity' per week. I exceed that minimum easily, especially if sex is included in the computation.

We were told that these next two years before we leave were years in which we would be prepared for life after school, whether at university or in a job. I remember the Head telling us a key element was that we should 'take responsibility for our studies' (I quote from my notes at the time) rather than simply following instructions from teachers. And also that we should 'use our initiative in self-directed study and extracurricular activities.'

These past six weeks I have taken responsibility for my exercise and used my initiative in self-directed sporting activities.

As this is what we were encouraged to do I see no reason to apologise for it.

But that is not the only explanation for missing your Wednesday sport.

I do not know, Mr. Pearson, Sir, if you were like me when you were my age. I doubt it somehow. I am one of those people who are always picked last for any team sport. It is true that I am not good at dashing about a sports field as if my life depended on it. (I know it doesn't.) I am not good at kicking a ball about with any skill. I am not good at 'tackling' other players with aggressive intent and a competitive desire to take the ball from them. I am hopeless at catching objects thrown at me. I am not bothered whether I win or lose at any game. In fact I find all forms of competitive physical activity repulsive. It seems to me to be a form of legitimised violence. I am against all forms of violence, most of all those invented in order merely to take exercise.

It is the people who are good at these things and like them who are appointed captains of sports teams, and choose the people to play with them. As I am known to be rubbish at the skills required, and because I make no secret of my dislike of competitive team games, it is no wonder I am only picked if there is no one else to make up the numbers. Mostly, during your sports afternoons, I am left out, unneeded, and spend the two and a half hours with the other leftovers, usually the same three or four of us, who are euphemistically and inaccurately called 'the reserves'.

I doubt, Mr. Pearson, Sir, that you have ever in your life been a leftover 'reserve'. You cannot therefore know the sense of humiliation felt by those of us who suffer this fate. You cannot know what it is like to muck about with two or three other rejects, aimlessly kicking a ball in a pretence of playing a game so as not to be shouted at from time to time by your good self, Sir. You cannot know how depressing this is on a cold and wet winter day. I would hope, though, Mr. Pearson, Sir, that you would at least appreciate, after giving it a few minutes' thought, what a waste of time this is. Time which I have decided, on my own initiative and taking responsibility for myself, to spend more valuably on my studies.

As I say, I cannot apologise for doing this.

Which brings me to the account you require of how I have spent my Wednesday afternoons for the past six weeks.

I can tell you that I spent them in the school library. The librarian will, I'm sure, confirm this.

But as I did not keep a diary of exactly what I accomplished during those afternoons, I cannot give you a detailed account. What I can tell you is that I spent the time doing self-directed study of extra-curricular subjects, viz: the sexual habits of the natterjack toad, the psychology and corruption of power in human activities (including sport), and the politics of passive resistance.

I will supply bibliographical references for the books consulted, if you require it.

To conclude, Mr. Pearson, Sir, I want to say that I regard sport as a peripheral activity in school life. It should not be allowed to take the place of the proper function of a school, which, in my humble opinion, is to educate young people in the study of human life through the arts and sciences. Taking exercise, which I agree is a wise thing to do, should take place outside school time in voluntary selection of the activities which most appeal to the individual and are best suited to his or her nature and aptitudes.

These are my reasons and explanations for not attending compulsory sports these last six weeks.

Yours sincerely,

Jason Hind.

To Head of School. Not only on the grounds of this pupil's nonattendance at compulsory sport, but also for the insulting tone of his letter and refusal to apologise for his misdemeanour, I recommend expulsion. If such behaviour and rudeness are allowed without a firm stand being taken we'll lose all authority and worse misdemeanours will spread like wildfire.

J.R.D. Pearson. Head of Sports.

To Head of Sports. Not accepted. I agree the boy was wrong in ducking out of a compulsory activity without speaking to you first, and I agree the sardonic tone and some of the content of his letter might be taken as an insult if one wants to look at it that way. But his point about our stated aims for the sixth form is well taken. We can't tell them to do something and then get upset when they do it.

I have seen Hind and given him a good talking to. I've instructed him to see you and apologise properly, and to attend on Wednesdays without fail. I made it clear that if he lapses I will review my decision not to expel him. However, I've also taken his point about the 'reserves'. (Perhaps you could do something better with those left out?) And have told him he may play indoor tennis with any of the other 'reserves' who may care to partner him.

That done, I suggest we let the matter drop.

W. P. Turnbull. Head of School.

The
Tower

'SURELY YOU UNDERSTAND NOW,' MR. PHELPS said, patient and smiling. 'I've explained it to you three times, Martin.'

His son sighed and stared at the Ordnance Survey map spread out on the camper table.

'I know,' he said. 'It's just that I'm sure there was a tower exactly where I've marked it.'

'You've got it wrong, nitwit. I keep telling you, there's a pond there, that's all.' The smile had gone now.

'I suppose.'

'What do you mean, you suppose!'

'But the map could be wrong. Or you could be wrong yourself.'

Mr. Phelps drew in his breath. 'Martin, there are times when I wonder if you have any brains at all. I've told you—I've seen it. The map is accurate and *I am not wrong!*'

'Don?' Mrs. Phelps was lying facedown on a picnic blanket spread on the grass just outside the camper door. 'Remember, dear, we're on holiday.' Though pretending to sleep as she sunbathed in her bikini, she had been eavesdropping on the conversation, half expecting it to end in a row.

Mr. Phelps shuffled from his seat behind the table and went to the door, his walking boots clumping on the floor and his angry weight making the camper tremble.

'Well,' he chuntered, 'he really is stupid as well as stubborn sometimes, Mary. I've explained till I'm blue in the face but he just doesn't seem capable of taking it in.'

'Maybe he has a blind spot for maps.'

'A blind spot for maps! Mary, you can't have a blind spot for maps. You can, perhaps, for French or maths. But not for maps. They're designed so any fool can understand.'

He stared across the heat-hazed field to the woods beyond and wondered why he hadn't gone off on his walk alone instead of listening to his son blathering about a tower that wasn't there and the map being wrong.

Mrs. Phelps flopped onto her back, put her sunglasses on and patted the rug at her side.

'Come and sit here for a few minutes,' she said.

Her husband obeyed, squatting cross-legged, his arms hugging his knees.

'I wouldn't mind,' he said, more in regret than anger now, 'if he just listened a bit more carefully. But he argues. Doesn't try to learn first.'

'It's his age,' Mrs. Phelps said. 'I bet you were just the same when you were fifteen.'

'Never!'

His wife laughed, gently. 'Course you were, everyone is.'

'Not me. I was keen to know about things. Everything. Information, that's what it's about. You don't get to know things by arguing the toss with someone who knows more than you do. You listen. Question. Pick their brains.'

Mrs. Phelps stroked her husband's knee. 'Well, you aren't in school now. Just relax. Enjoy yourself. That's what holidays are for.'

Mr. Phelps edged his legs out of range of his wife's hand.

The summer afternoon sang.

'Maybe,' Mrs. Phelps said after a while, but quietly so that Martin wouldn't hear, 'maybe we should have let him go off with his friends after all.'

'Camping with a bunch of yobs? Not on!'

'You're too hard on him.'

'He'll appreciate it later.'

'At his age you need some freedom, Don. A life of your own.'

'Ho!' Mr. Phelps snorted. 'Freedom to act like an idiot, you mean. Freedom to roam the streets and vandalize bus shelters. Freedom to terrorize old people and mess yourself up with drugs. Some freedom that is!'

'What makes you think Martin would behave like that?'

'Oh, come on, Mary. You've seen the rubbish who hang around our place. I passed a gang of them the other night. Half of them smoking their heads off while they watched the other half make a meal of the local females. About which enough said!'

Mrs. Phelps sighed. 'That's a kind of learning too, I suppose.'

Her husband flicked a hand at a bombarding fly. 'Well, as far as I'm concerned, it's a lesson Martin can do without, thanks.'

For a few moments neither spoke.

Mr. Phelps whisked at more attacking flies, but with less ferocity now.

'Why not go for your walk?' Mrs. Phelps said when she was sure the storm had blown over.

Her husband stood up in one smooth movement without using his hands. 'Perhaps I will.' He tucked his shirt in and hitched his trousers. 'There's a long barrow just north of us. No record of it being excavated. I'll poke about there for a while. Might be interesting.'

He collected his stick from the back of the car, said, 'See you in a couple of hours,' and stalked away.

From his seat in the camper Martin watched his father stride across the field, climb the gate in the hedge and disappear up the lane. Then he returned his gaze to the map lying on the table at his elbows. A week ago he had been looking at it with excited anticipation. Now he regarded it with distaste. Nothing ever turned out as well as you hoped.

He slipped out from behind the table, took an apple from the basket in the food cupboard, bit into its juicy crispness, went to the door and sat on the step, his feet square on the ground.

The noise of his munching was loud in the country silence.

'Enjoying it?' his mother said.

Martin nodded, knowing she was watching from behind her shades.

'He'll feel better after his walk,' Mrs. Phelps said.

Martin nodded again.

He gnawed his apple to the core, then lobbed it high over his mother's body to fall in the long grass beyond. From where it landed a small dark bird he didn't recognize flew up, startled. If his father had still been here, he would have insisted that he look it up in his recognition book.

'Could I help?' Mrs. Phelps asked.

'Doubt it,' Martin said, squinting as he tried to follow the bird's flight into the sun.

Mrs. Phelps sat up and turned to face him. 'Won't you tell me what the trouble is?'

'Doesn't matter.'

'You were having quite a set-to for something that doesn't matter.'

Martin shrugged. 'It's just that I say the map is wrong, and Dad says I don't know how to read it properly.'

Mrs. Phelps took her sunglasses off. 'What do you say is wrong?'

Martin sighed. 'You know how he set me a route to walk this morning to prove I could use the map on my own?'

'Yes.'

'Well, I managed all right really. Just missed a couple of details. Only little things. But on the last leg down Tinkley Lane—'

'The one that runs along the far side of this field?'

'Yes. There's a quarry along there, about a mile away, and a benchmark, and a couple of disused farm buildings, and I got them all OK.'

'But?'

'In a field with a pond in it about three quarters of a mile away—four sixths, actually, to be exact—I saw a tower.'

'And?'

'It isn't marked on the map so I put it in.'

'But Dad says it isn't there?'

Martin nodded.

Mrs. Phelps put her sunglasses on again. 'But, sweetheart, I don't see the problem. Either the tower is there or it isn't.'

'That's what we were rowing about.'

Mrs. Phelps laughed. 'Men! Why row? Why not just go and find out together?'

'I wanted to. But Dad wouldn't.' Martin stood up. 'He said he knew it wasn't there. He said he'd been along that way twice already since we got here and he'd never seen a tower. But I know it's there, Mum, I saw it this morning for certain.'

'All right, all right!' Agitation in her son's voice warned that care was needed. 'Come here. Sit down. Let's have that shirt off. Get some sunlight on you. You're as bad as your dad. You both think you'll evaporate if you get sun on your skin.'

Reluctantly, Martin tugged his shirt off and sat so that his mother could rub sun oil onto his back.

'This tower,' she said as she anointed him, 'what did it look like?'

'A bit weird really. Built of stone and quite high. Fifteen metres. Twenty maybe. And it was round. With little slit windows, and pointed tops like in a church. But there wasn't a spire or anything, the roof was flat, with battlements round the edge like a castle. There was a biggish doorway at the bottom, with an arch like the windows. But there was no door. And the wall was partly covered in ivy, and weeds and even clumps of flowers were growing out of the cracks between some of the stones.'

'How exciting. Lie down and I'll do your front.'

'No, I'll do myself.'

Martin took the tube and began oiling his chest.

'Did you go inside?'

'I started pacing towards it because I wanted to try and fix its position on the map exactly. But after thirty paces, well before I even reached the pond . . . I don't know . . . the air went chilly. Just all of a sudden. Like I'd come up against a wall of cold.'

He stopped rubbing the oil and looked at his mother's masked eyes.

'Made me feel a bit scared. Don't know why. There weren't any cattle in the field, nothing to be scared of, you know. But I stopped pacing and just stood. And then I noticed how quiet the place was. I mean quiet in an odd sort of way.'

Martin paused, his eyes now not focused, though he was looking straight at his mother.

'And what was so odd?' Mrs. Phelps said as calmly as she could.

Martin's eyes focused again.

'No birds,' he said. 'None flying anywhere near and not a sound of any birdsong either. Not even insects. Nothing. Just dead silence.'

Mother and son stared at each other.

'Perhaps a kestrel lives in the tower? Or some other bird of prey?'

Martin shook his head.

'You can't be sure.'

'Can.'

'How?'

'Went in.'

'Even though you were scared?'

'I'm trying to tell you!'

'All right, OK, I'm listening.'

'It was pretty hot this morning, right?'

His mother nodded.

'A heat haze, just like now?'

'Was there?'

'I didn't notice either till I was in the field. I'd noticed about the birds and was looking at the tower. It seemed normal, just an old stone building, you know. The field all around is long grass, like this one, with a tall hedge, and a wood opposite from the lane side. And it was while I was looking at the wood that it hit me.'

He stopped, uncertain of himself.

'Go on, sweetheart,' Mrs. Phelps said.

'Well, everything, the wood and the hedge and the grass in the field, even the pond—everything was shimmering in the haze. But the tower . . . It wasn't. It was quite still. The shape of it was clear-cut.'

Mrs. Phelps gave an involuntary shudder. She didn't really believe Martin's story. Not that he would lie. He never lied. But he did get carried away by his imagination sometimes. Even so—a tower standing cold and silent in the middle of a summer field. She shuddered again. Curious how a few words, just by association, can chill you on a lovely day in hot sunshine.

She came back to herself. Martin was still telling his story and she had missed something. She said, 'Sorry, darling, I was distracted. What did you say?'

'The tower,' Martin said. 'It was cool inside, wonderfully cool, and restful.'

'Wasn't it locked up?'

'No, I told you. There was a doorway but no door. I went straight in. And inside the place was smelly, really stank, like empty places often do, don't they, as if people have used them for lavatories. But it was quite clean, no rubbish or anything. A round-shaped room with a bare earth floor. And one of the little pointed windows with no glass in it. And a stone stairway that started just inside the door and curled up round the wall to a floor above. No banister, just the stone stairs in the wall.'

'No sign of life?'

'Nothing. Deserted. And very cool. Really nice after the heat. Well, anyway, I thought it must have a terrific view from the top, so I climbed the stairs. Thirty-two. Counted them. Eighteen to the second floor, and fourteen to the top. The first floor was just old wooden boards. A few bird droppings but nothing else.'

'And safe. Not rotten or anything?'

'No. I wouldn't have gone on if it hadn't been safe, would I? I'm not that stupid, whatever Dad thinks.'

'It's just his manner. So was there a good view?'

'Not really. After the field there's trees in the way in most directions. But it was nice. There's a parapet so you can't fall off. And it was just as cool up there as inside. I'd have stayed longer, but I knew if I didn't get home in reasonable time, Dad would start getting at me for taking so long to do a simple route. So I came down, paced the distance back to the lane, marked the position on the map, and came back.'

Mrs. Phelps took a deep breath. 'What a story!'

Martin glared at her. 'It is not a story. It's what happened.'

His mother leaned to him and hugged his face to hers. 'Yes, my love, I know,' she said. 'I mean, what a strange thing to find a tower like that and it not be on the map.'

Martin pulled free. 'Don't you start!'

Mrs. Phelps leaned back on her hands. 'Did you tell your father all this?'

Martin grimaced in disdain.

'No,' his mother said. 'Best not to, I suppose.'

'He wouldn't believe me about the tower being there. So you know what he'd say about the rest. Rubbish, he'd say, pure imagination.'

Mrs. Phelps thought for a while then stood up and adjusted her bikini. 'Look, why don't I slip into something respectable and you can show me your tower? That'll settle matters.'

Martin shook his head.

'Why not? If I've seen it he can't go on saying it isn't there.'

'But that'll only make it worse. He'll get angry and say we ganged up against him, that I got you to take my side, that I can't stand on my own feet.'

Impasse.

After thinking for a moment Mrs. Phelps said, 'I'll tell you what. You go on your own, and double-check the position of the tower. After all, you just might have made a mistake. Then come back and tell me. After supper this evening, I'll suggest we take a walk, and I'll make sure we go along Tinkley Lane past the tower. That way, we'll all see it together and your father won't be able to say you're wrong. How about that?'

Martin considered.

'OK,' he said, cheering up. 'But I know it's where I said it was.'

''Cause it is, my love. But make sure. And while you're gone I'll fix supper so that everything's ready when your father gets back.'

Martin pulled on his shirt, collected his map from the camper, folded it so he could hold it easily and see the area round the tower, gave his mother a tentative hug, and set off across the field.

Mrs. Phelps watched her son out of sight before going inside, pulling on a pair of jeans and an old shirt of her husband's, and slipping her feet into her sandals.

Martin sauntered down the lane, stifled by the heat cocooned between the high, dense hedgerows. Wasps and flies whirred past his head. A yellowhammer *pink-pink*ed behind him. Straight above, crawling across the dazzling blue, a speck of airplane spun its white spider thread.

His shirt clung uncomfortably to his oiled body. He glanced up the lane and down, and, seeing no one, tugged the shirt off and used it as a fly-whisk as he walked along. Usually he kept covered, too embarrassed by his scrawny build to show himself in public. Boys at school called him Needle.

Even without his shirt he was sweating by the time he reached the gateless opening in the hedge that led to the tower. And sure enough, there it was, looking just as it had in the morning. This time he noticed at once how coldly it stood and clearly outlined while all around grass and flowers and trees and rocks and even the pond at the foot of the tower shimmered in the haze. And while he looked, just as that morning, he felt a nerve-tingling strangeness. He tried to work out what the strangeness was and decided it was like knowing something was going to happen to you but not quite knowing what.

There must, Martin thought, be some ordinary explanation. His father would probably know what it was, and would tell him, if only he would stop insisting that the tower wasn't there, and come and see for himself while the heat haze was still rising. By this evening, when his mother tricked his father into seeing the tower, the haze would have vanished.

As he checked its position on his map, Martin remembered the coolness and how much he had wanted to stay in the tower. Now there was nothing to hurry back to the camper for. He could stay and enjoy himself. He might even make a den, a secret place where he could come and be by himself during the rest of the week. He could properly explore the building. There was bound to be something interesting if he looked carefully enough. There was also the pond. There might be fish to be caught. And if he wanted to sunbathe, the tower roof was a good place. No one could see him lying behind the parapet, but he would be able to spy anyone approaching across the field. He might even go home after the holiday with a useful tan.

He was about to enter the field when he heard a shout. A cry, in fact, rather than a yell. A girl's voice, high-pitched and desperate. Coming from the direction of the tower.

Shading his eyes with a hand, he searched the tower but could see no one.

The cry came again.

And suddenly he knew what caused the strangeness he felt.

It was as if he had been waiting for this cry, that it had reached him as a sensation long before he heard it as a sound in his ears.

As he stared with unblinking eyes, he saw a girl's head, then her body appear above the parapet till she was revealed to her waist. She was about fifteen or sixteen and wearing a sleeveless white summer-loose dress. But from this distance it was difficult to see her features clearly, which anyway were partly hidden by long dark hair that fell around her face and shoulders.

She grasped the wall of the parapet with one hand. The other she raised above her head and waved urgently at Martin.

At first he thought she was only excited, perhaps pretending to be frightened by the height. But then she cried out again in that high-pitched urgent voice.

She seemed to be shouting, 'Come back, come back!' and waving him towards her.

But that could not be. He had never seen her before.

Puzzled, Martin did not move, except to raise his own hand and wave back in a polite reflex action.

Still the girl waved and cried, 'Come back, come back!'

She's mistaken me for someone else, Martin thought. But even as he thought this, smoke began to drift up from the tower behind the girl, first only a thin blue smudge in the air, which quickly became a thicker feathering, and then, after a belching puff, a dense, curling ribbon that streamed straight up into the sky, grey-white against the deep blue.

As the smoke thickened, the girl's cries became more panic-stricken, her hand-waving more frantic.

Which at last brought Martin to life again.

Dropping his shirt and map, he sprinted towards the tower.

Mrs. Phelps gave her son a few minutes' start before setting off after him. But she got no farther than the gate when she met her husband striding down the lane towards her. She knew at once that he was excited from the jaunty way he was windmilling his stick.

'You'll never guess,' he said as he approached.

'What?' Mrs. Phelps grinned, expecting some story about her husband finding an almost extinct flower or spotting a rare bird.

'Just been talking to an old farmer. Asked him if he knew of a stone tower anywhere in the district.' He paused, enjoying the drama.

'And?'

'At first he said no. Nothing of that sort round here, sir!' Mr. Phelps, who prided himself on his talent for mimicry, imitated the farmer's accent. 'Then he remembered. Ah, wait a minute, sir, he says, yes there were one. But that were years back, sir, when I were a boy, like.'

Mrs. Phelps caught at her breath.

Her husband went on, unaware. 'I quizzed him — without letting on about Martin, of course. Apparently, there used to be an old teasel tower where the pond is just down the lane from here. You know the sort. You always say they look as if they're straight out of a fairy tale. *Sleeping Beauty*, *Rapunzel* and all that rubbish. And I came across a teasel growing wild this morning when I was checking on Martin's nonexistent tower. Rather like a tall thistle, with a large very prickly head. Well, it was the heads they dried in those towers and then used them for raising the nap on cloth. Fascinating process.'

'Yes, darling, but—?'

'They cut the dried heads in two and attached them to a cylinder which revolved against the cloth so that the prickles snagged against the fabric just sufficiently to scuff the surface.' Mr. Phelps chuckled. 'Teasing it, you might say.'

'Don—'

'And do you know, Mary, they still haven't been able to invent a machine that can do the job better. Isn't that extraordinary!'

'Don, the tower—what did the old man tell you?'

'I'm just coming to that. According to the old chap, one day during a long hot summer like this, the tower burned to the ground.'

'Burned—?'Mrs. Phelps flinched.

'Hang on, that isn't all. A young girl is supposed to have died in the blaze. The old chap told a marvellous tale about how she was meeting her boyfriend there in secret and somehow the fire started, no one ever found out how, and the girl got trapped.'

'Don, listen —'

'The boyfriend ran off, scared he'd be caught with the girl, I expect. You know how strict they were in those days about that sort of thing, and quite right too. The wretched boy deserted her, poor lass, and she died in the flames. Young love betrayed by cowardice.'

'He's gone there,' Mrs. Phelps said bleakly.

'A nice yarn but all nonsense, of course. However, it does look as if there might have been a tower somewhere near where Martin thought he saw one. Isn't that odd!'

Mrs. Phelps turned away and set off at a jog down the lane.

'Hang on, Mary,' Mr. Phelps called after her. 'Haven't finished yet.'

'Got to find him,' his wife called back.

'But wait!' Mr. Phelps waved his stick. 'I want Martin to take us to where he thought he saw the tower.'

Without turning, Mrs. Phelps shouted back, her voice carrying her panic, 'He's gone there already!'

Hearing at last what his wife was saying, Mr. Phelps sprinted after her, ungainly in his walking boots.

'Gone there?' he called as he ran.

'To check. We must catch him.'

'Steady! Wait!'

By the time Mr. Phelps reached his wife he was almost speechless from lack of breath. He seized her arm and pulled her to a stop.

'Mary, you're being hysterical. What is all this?'

'Can't you see?' Mrs. Phelps panted. 'Martin wasn't wrong.'

'Having us on!'

'No! There! To him, it was *there*!'

'Rubbish!' Mr. Phelps leaned forward, both hands on his stick, recovering his breath. 'He'd found out. Only pretending he'd seen it. Some kind of joke.'

'No, no, no!' Mrs. Phelps was near to tears with desperation.

Her husband glared at her. 'Pull yourself together, Mary, for heaven's sake!'

As if she had been slapped, his wife's tears suddenly gave way to anger. She glared fiercely back at her husband.

'Don't you speak to me like that, Don! Don't you dare condescend to me! You think you know everything. To you the world is just one big museum of plain straightforward facts. Well, let me tell you, you don't know everything. There's more to this world than your boring facts! And for once I don't care what you think. I believe Martin saw that tower. He's gone back there. And I'm going after him. I'm afraid what might happen if he sees it again. Call that a mother's intuition. Call it what you like. But I *feel* it. That's all I know. Now, are you coming or aren't you?'

Mr. Phelps stood open-mouthed and rigid with astonishment at his wife's outburst.

By the time Martin reached the tower, smoke was billowing from every window and crevice.

Instinctively bending almost double, he ran inside.

The force of the air being sucked in through the doorway pressed against his bare back like a firm hand pushing him on.

At once he found himself engulfed in blinding, choking fumes, could hear the roar of flames from across the room, could feel their blistering heat on his skin.

But still from above came the girl's panic-stricken cries.

Without thought or care, he threw himself to the left and onto the stairs. He pounded up them, stumbling, coughing. Hardly able to see for smoke, he kept his left hand pressed against the wall for fear of veering to the edge of the stairs and falling into the furnace on the floor below, from where flames were already leaping high enough to lick the exposed floorboards of the room above. He held his right arm against his face, trying to protect it from the scorching blaze.

On the second floor flames were already eating at the boards. The dry wood was crackling; small explosions were sending showers of sparks cascading across the room. And, mingled with the suffocating fumes, the stench of burning flesh was so strong that Martin retched as he staggered on hands and feet now up the second flight of stairs. By the time he reached the trapdoor to the roof he was choking for breath, his smoke-filled eyes were streaming with tears and all down his right side he felt as if his skin were being peeled from him like paint being stripped by a blowtorch.

The tower had become one giant, roaring chimney.

Martin hauled himself up into the air, gulping for breath. Once on the roof he clung for a moment to the parapet, unable to move till he recovered his strength. But he knew there was no time to spare.

Through tear-blurred eyes and the fog of smoke swirling about him, he looked round for the girl and saw her only an arm's length away still waving and crying desperately in the direction of the road.

'Here!' he tried to shout. 'I'm here!'

But the words clogged in his parched throat.

So he reached out to take her by the shoulders and turn her to him.

'Surely we're nearly there!' Mrs. Phelps panted.

Clumping along beside her, Mr. Phelps, breathless too and sweating, said, 'That beech tree. Just there.'

Seconds later Mrs. Phelps spotted her son's shirt and map lying in the road.

'Don!' she cried, rushing to pick them up. 'They're Martin's!'

She turned and saw the gap in the hedge, and dashed towards it. But her husband, arriving at the same instant, pushed her aside and ran ahead into the field, causing Mrs. Phelps to fall to her knees.

'Oh, God!' she pleaded, and, finding her feet again, stumbled after him.

'Martin!' Mr. Phelps was calling when both he and his wife were brought to a sudden stop.

Across the field, high above the pond, they saw their son floating upright in the air, his arms outstretched as if reaching for something.

'Dear Lord!' Mr. Phelps muttered.

But neither he nor his wife could move. Spellbound, they could do no more than watch as their son took hold of that invisible something for which he was reaching and clutched it eagerly to him in a passionate embrace. For a long moment he remained like that, his body utterly still, until, suddenly, he opened his arms wide, peered down and, in a strangely slow, dreamlike movement, as if from a high diving board, launched himself earthwards.

The instant Martin's body hit the water, Mrs. Phelps came violently alive.

'Martin!' she screamed, and hurtled across the field.

Her scream seemed to bring her husband back to his senses. He sprinted after her, yelling, 'Mary . . . Mary . . . Careful!'

But Mrs. Phelps paid him no heed. By the time she reached the pond her son's body had surfaced and was floating facedown in the middle. She plunged in headlong, her arms flailing, but found herself at once entangled in clinging weeds that grew around the edge.

Galloping up behind her, Mr. Phelps made no attempt to swim, but ploughed in till he was wading waist-high towards his son, his frantic strides churning the water to froth and his boots so disturbing the stagnant mud on the pond's bottom that it belched up great bubbles of putrid gas in his trail.

As soon as they had lifted Martin onto the bank Mr. Phelps said, 'Leave him to me!' And with a sureness and skill that surprised his wife, began reviving their son with the kiss of life.

It was only when Martin was breathing properly again that Mrs. Phelps noticed the ugly blisters covering the right side of his body. She was sitting with Martin's head cradled in her lap and had been going to cover him with his shirt. Instead she looked at her husband who was kneeling at her side and saw that he too had seen the burns.

'We must get him to hospital,' she said, working hard to keep the shock from sounding in her voice.

Mr. Phelps nodded.

Martin opened his eyes. 'Mum,' he said.

'Hush, sweetheart. It's all right. You're safe now.'

Martin blinked in the bright sunlight, and coughed up water.

His mother eased his position, holding him so that he could breathe easily.

'Is the girl all right?' Martin asked when the spasm was over.

His parents glanced at each other.

'She'll be fine,' his mother said, smiling down at him.

Martin tried to raise himself. 'Where is she?' he asked.

His mother gently restrained him. 'She's been taken care of. Don't worry.'

'You see, Martin—' his father began.

'Not yet,' Mrs. Phelps said as lightly as she could. 'Later.'

Her husband turned away. 'I'd better get the car and take you to hospital, old son,' he said.

Martin said, 'I told you it was there, Dad, didn't I?'

Mr. Phelps peered across the empty field hidden from his son by his wife's cradling body.

'You did,' he said.

'And I got the position exactly on the map.'

'You certainly did. Well done!'

Mr. Phelps looked down at his son and stared into his eyes for the first time in months. And the boy's gaze, looking frankly back at him, as though somehow he now knew all there was to know about his father, caused Mr. Phelps to shudder.

Mrs. Phelps observed her husband's discomfort and felt his pain. But there was nothing she could do to help him. The time for that had passed. And their holiday too was over.

'We ought to get him away from here as soon as we can,' she said gently.

Mr. Phelps took a deep breath and braced himself. 'I'll only be a jiffy,' he said, and set off towards the lane at a steady jog.

Mrs. Phelps watched him go and suddenly felt utterly exhausted. The sun was scorching her back, but she knew she mustn't move. The warmth reminded her that Martin had said how cool it had been near the tower. It certainly wasn't now. And all around grasshoppers rasped. She listened. There was also plenty of bird noise and the loud skirl of passing flies and bees. None of the strange silence he'd mentioned.

Martin broke in on her thoughts. 'Am I badly hurt?'

'Not badly,' his mother said, brushing scorched hair from his forehead.

'Was I out for long?'

'Long enough.'

'Has the tower burned down completely?'

'Afraid so.'

'That's a pity. It was a nice place. But the girl's OK?'

'I'm sure she is,' Mrs. Phelps said with utter conviction. 'Thanks to you.'

'And I will see her again, won't I?'

'Would you like to?'

'Wouldn't mind.' Martin grinned sheepishly at his mother. 'She was quite pretty really.'

'Yes,' Mrs. Phelps said, struggling against tears. 'I expect she was.'

Up *for It*

GREG AND JOSH ARE SITTING ON A PARK BENCH *after work as junior shelf-fillers at a local supermarket. A schoolgirl in sports outfit walks by and sits down on the next park bench.*

> *Greg:* She looks up for it.
>
> *Josh:* Yeah, she's up for it.
>
> *Greg:* Definitely up for it.
>
> *Josh:* I'm up for it as well.
>
> *Greg:* You're always up for it.
>
> *Josh:* You can talk.
>
> *Greg:* So when did you last have it?
>
> *Josh:* I'm not talking about having it.
>
> *Greg:* No. But when?
>
> *Josh:* I'm talking about being up for it.
>
> *Greg:* But when did you last have it?
>
> *Josh:* When did you?

Greg: Last night, as it happens.

Josh: Last night?

Greg: I had it last night.

Josh: I was with you last night and you didn't have it when I was with you.

Greg: But I wasn't with you all of last night, was I?

Josh: Who then? Who did you have it with when I wasn't with you last night?

Greg: Her from Panini.

Josh: Her? Her from Panini? From behind the counter at Panini?

Greg: Yeah. Her. So?

Josh: She'll have it with anybody.

Greg: Have you had it with her?

Josh: No! No, I have not. Wouldn't touch it with a bargepole.

Greg: What about you, then? When did you last have it?

Josh: I wouldn't have it with her from the Panini, no sweat.

Greg: Come on then. When?

Josh: Her over there.

Greg: You haven't had it with her.

Josh: No, course not!

Greg: What about her, then?

Josh: She hasn't done nothing.

Greg: True.

Josh: Not one glance.

Greg: Not a glance.

Josh: I don't think she's up for it, d'you?

Greg: Nah. Not up for it at all, she ain't.

Josh: Too stuck up.

Greg: Too nose in the air.

(Pause)

Josh: You up for a panini?

Greg: Yeah, wouldn't mind.

Josh: Panini then, yeah?

Greg: Yeah, OK. Panini.

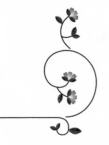

The God Debate

SCENE ONE

TWO BOARDING SCHOOL BOYS SIT ON A BENCH *in the school garden. They have just been taught about debating by their English teacher.*

> *Hamish:* Do you miss your mother?
>
> *Henry:* No.
>
> *Hamish:* Your father?
>
> *Henry:* Not really.
>
> *Hamish:* Who do you miss?
>
> *Henry:* I miss God.
>
> *Hamish:* God?
>
> *Henry:* Yes, God.
>
> *Hamish:* Who is God?
>
> *Henry:* I don't know.
>
> *Hamish:* How can you miss someone you don't know?

Henry: I don't know. I just do.

Hamish: But you know your mother?

Henry: Yes.

Hamish: And your father.

Henry: Yes, of course.

Hamish: But you don't know God.

Henry: No.

Hamish: And you miss him.

Henry: Yes.

Hamish: Why?

Henry: I don't know.

Hamish: How do you know you miss God, then?

Henry: Because I think about him.

Hamish: How do you know God's a he if you don't know who God is?

Henry: I didn't say God was a he. You said he was a he. You said and I quote, God's a he if you don't know who God is.

Hamish: Well, you know what I mean.

Henry: No, I don't. Actually, I don't really know what I mean either.

Hamish: But you miss God.

Henry: Yes.

Hamish (*peeling a banana*): Is there anything I can do to help you, then?

Henry: You could stop talking.

Hamish: How would that help?

Henry: Then I could think.

Hamish: What would you think about?

Henry: I'd think about God.

Hamish: But you've said that when you think about him you miss him so how would that help?

Henry: Well, I feel closer to God when I miss God than when I don't think about God. So if you wouldn't mind—

Hamish: I don't mind.

Henry: That's the difference probably.

Hamish: The difference?

Henry: Between you and God. You and everyone, my mother, my father, between everyone and God. God minds.

Hamish: I mind.

Henry: You've just said you didn't mind.

Hamish: I meant that I didn't mind not talking.

Henry: Good. Well, as I say, that would help. You not talking.

Hamish: All right, then.

SCENE TWO

Hamish: Better?

Henry: Yes, much better, thank you.

Hamish: Have you found God yet?

Henry: No, but I feel better.

Hamish: I don't.

Henry: That's because you like talking all the time.

Hamish: No, I don't.

Henry: You do. You just said you didn't mind being quiet a little while ago.

Hamish: I don't.

Henry: Well, do then.

Hamish: Do what?

Henry: Be quiet.

Hamish: All right.

SCENE THREE

Hamish: Better?

Henry: Yes, a bit better now. Quiet is good, isn't it?

(Pause)

Hamish: It has a peace about it, you're right.

Henry: It's you who's right this time. Peace is the word.

Hamish: Peace is good, don't you think?

Henry: Better than my mother, at any rate. And my father, thinking about it.

Hamish: Peace.

Henry: Peace.

(Pause)

Henry: Perhaps that's what God is, then?

Hamish: Sounds about right.

(Pause)

Hamish: I'm hungry now. Are you?

Henry: Yes, starving.

Hamish: Not too hungry for God to eat?

Henry: Course not.

SCENE FOUR

Cook: You've missed lunch. Twenty minutes too late. Everything's been cleared away.

Hamish: But we're starving.

Cook: You know the rule. It's your responsibility to be on time for meals.

Henry: But it's not God-given, is it?

Cook: Is what?

Henry: The rule. About being late.

Cook: What about the rule? I haven't a clue what you're jabbering about.

Henry: What I mean is, if they're not God-given, they're only human and they can be changed, can't they?

Cook: I don't know about God but I do know the school rules. I don't make them. The Head does. You want them changed, go and talk to him.

Hamish: Can't we have even a sandwich?

Cook: We're clearing away now.

Hamish: You said everything had already been cleared away.

Cook: It has.

Henry: But if you're still clearing away, how can —

Cook: Enough! We're busy and you're late. End of story. Skedaddle!

SCENE FIVE

Hamish and Henry return to their bench in the school garden.

Henry: Blast!

Hamish: Well, you shouldn't have gone on about God!

Henry: I was only telling you that I missed him.

Hamish: Well, now we've both missed lunch.

Henry: Never mind, there's always the tuck shop.

Hamish: Closed.

Henry: Back to God then.

Hamish: I'm sick of God.

Henry: I'm not sick of him. I'm God-sick. Two different things.

Hamish: You're definitely sick anyway.

Henry: No, I'm not. I say though, what happened to that banana you had earlier?

Hamish: Oh, that. Yes. Sorry. Ate it while I wasn't talking so you could think about God.

The Kissing Game

H<small>E WONDERED IF HE WOULD EVER SPEAK TO</small> her again.

On past experience, probably not.

Shyness, he thought, not for the first time, should be treated as an illness. For years people had been telling him he'd grow out of it. Now, almost seventeen, he still hadn't. In fact, he suffered worse than ever.

Another wasted opportunity, he told himself with familiar self-punishing anger. Like the one last week in the High Street with Sue Pritchard, and the one before that in the drama studio with Ellen Mitchell (who everyone said was a doddle to chat up), and the one before that with Jane Carpenter in the underpass when there wasn't even anyone else around to put him off, and the one before that and that and that.

He slammed the back door behind him and instantly, blushing as usual, regretted it. If she were still there she'd hear, think him a blunderer, and laugh.

Had she not taken him by surprise (or, more accurately, he taken her), he'd never have spoken to her at all. He didn't know she was lying there sunbathing. He'd only climbed the tree to dismantle what remained of his childhood tree house, something his father had been on about for weeks.

'You don't use it now,' his father kept saying. 'You've grown out of it. The damn thing's an eyesore, especially in winter. And it's dangerous as well. If any of it falls on someone next door I'll be sued for damages.'

That morning his father had given an ultimatum.

'Take it down pronto or you don't get the new laptop for your birthday.'

So after his parents had left for work he took a hammer and climbed to the rickety platform and began bashing at the slats of the tree house walls only to hear startled cries from below, on the other side of the fence. Peering through the high-summer foliage, he saw her sitting on a beach towel and staring up at him in alarm.

'Sorry,' he called. 'Didn't, didn't know you were, were there.'

'What!' She jumped up, her arms crossed over her chest, but was blinded by the sun and had to raise a hand to shade her eyes. 'Who are you? What are you doing?'

'It's all right.'

'What?'

It was then he dropped the hammer, which hit a branch, bounced, clipped the top of the fence, and landed with a dull thud at her feet.

She screamed and jumped back, tripped and fell.

'Just my ham, hammer,' he called, already scrambling down, and swung from the lowest branch, as he used to when he was a kid, into the next-door garden to retrieve it. Only then did he think this might not have been the best way of dealing with the situation.

He held the hammer, showing it to her, grinning, in what he knew must seem an inane fashion, while she stood on the other side of the towel trembling, crossed hands holding her upper arms, staring at him.

'I'm from next door,' he said, the stupidity of which struck him even as he said it. He pointed the hammer, with equal stupidity, at the tree. 'Taking down an old, an old tree house.'

His throat seized up.

They were both speechless.

At last she said, not without difficulty, 'I was sunbathing.'

He nodded, aware of her unclothed skin, of all her body, almost in reach. He even thought he could feel warmth coming off her. She seemed to glow. The sight was dumbfounding. Waves of shyness engulfed him, the old enemy. He dropped his eyes, shuffled his feet, could think of no savvy way to stay or go.

Hating himself for his pathetic affliction, he turned, awkwardly climbed the fence, went into the house, slamming the back door.

For the rest of the day embarrassment jailed him inside.

The picture of her, seen from the tree, came back to him in bed that night, provoking an agony of yearning. He rewrote reality. Now she did not sit up startled, but lay in the sun, inviting him to join her. He craned down smoothly to the ground. She stood to greet him. He tracked into close-up. Hands on her hair. On her face. On her body. Looking at her mouth. Her eyes. Her eyes said yes.

No question, he had to do something about her. Couldn't go on forever, never, not with anyone. He'd go mad. But do what?

The thing was to make some sort of contact, anyhow, so long as it didn't require him to speak first. Somehow make her come to him, speak to him. That would be a start, another chance at least. But how?

He was quite good with words, everyone at school said so. As long as they were written down. If he had to say them to people he didn't know, and especially to girls he fancied, he couldn't get them out or they came out bumbled. At worst, he stammered.

But on paper . . .

Next morning, after his parents had gone, he put his night-formed plan into action.

He wrote:

> Sorry about yesterday. Didn't mean to disturb you. The hammer was an accident. Wasn't trying to brain you! The thing is my dad wants me to get rid of the tree house from the tree that overhangs your garden. I have to do it this week. But I don't want to stop you sunbathing or anything. If you could let me know when you won't be using the garden I'll do it then. I'll be at home all day today if you want to call with an answer.
> Thanks.
> James Taggart.

He wasn't sure about the opening. Not knowing who the girl was—he had never seen her before; she must be a visitor—he didn't know what to call her. And there wasn't much contact between the two houses, both sides pretty much keeping to themselves—polite and cooperative when necessary, but not what anyone would call close neighbours except in the geographical sense. So he hadn't heard about her coming.

The note would have to do, he couldn't waste all day on it. He slipped it into an envelope and addressed it to The Girl in the Garden.

The next problem was delivery. He knew that the Bells, who lived there, both went out to work. But if he pushed it through the letterbox himself, she might see him, come to the door and ask what he wanted, and he couldn't handle that. He considered the possibility of keeping watch to see if she left the house and delivering the note then. But what if she didn't go out? Or to see if she went into the garden— to sunbathe perhaps—and nipping round then. But the thought of her sunbathing revived his nighttime fantasy of their sunbathing together and made him desperate to be in touch.

It was then he heard the postman, thought of a solution, sprinted to the door before he could consider what he was doing and called the postman back.

'Wrong address?'

'I've got a letter.'

'Congratulations.'

'I mean, would you take it?'

'Only deliver, don't collect, sorry, son. Put it in the box.'

'For next door.'

The postman laughed. 'Take it yourself.'

'. . . a surprise.'

'Some sort of gag?'

'Just a note. Don't want her to see, to see me.'

'Oh, like that, is it! You're sure it's nothing nasty?'

'Just a note.'

'Yes, well—OK, this once.'

The postman took it, tutting and shaking his head.

The rest of the morning was miserable. Nothing happened. He prowled between his parents' upstairs front bedroom, from where he could keep an eye on any comings and goings next door, and the back landing window, which overlooked their garden. She did not come out. The sun stayed in. Now and then he wandered into his own garden hoping she might come and speak to him. But no. Neither sight nor sound. The place might as well have been deserted.

While he was scoffing beans on toast about one o'clock the telephone rang.

'Hello? This is Rosie Bell . . . The girl in the garden?'

'Oh—yes!'

'About your letter . . . I won't be out today . . . There's no sun. As you probably noticed.'

'No. I me, mean yes!'

'So it's all right to do your tree house.'

'Thanks.'

'OK . . . Bye.'

The dial tone sounded before he could reply. He slammed the receiver down and swore. If only he'd known she'd do that, he'd have prepared something to say. Now he'd messed up another chance. Damn, damn, damn.

For the rest of the afternoon he slumped in front of the television only half attending while in his head by turns rewriting the telephone script so that he came out of it better and mentally flogging himself for not having done so.

At dinner that evening his father said, 'No progress on the Tarzan residence, then.'

'Very funny, Dad.'

'I meant what I said.'

'I was going to do it yesterday but there was a girl sunbathing next, next, next door.'

'Which reminds me,' his mother said quickly with the extra cheerfulness she injected into her voice at such dangerous moments, 'I met Mrs. Harding this morning.'

'Beech Grove's own double agent,' his father said, predictably.

'According to her, the girl is the Bells' niece. Donald Bell's brother's daughter, Rosie.'

'A stunner is she, Jim?'

'From London,' his mother said.

'Big city girl. Watch yourself, Jim!'

'She's here for a change, apparently, a sort of holiday. Mrs. Harding thought there was a health problem.'

'Hard luck, Jim, steer clear.'

'Oh, it's all right, nothing to worry about. Nothing catching. Emotional apparently. One of the phobias.'

'Like my Hardingphobia, you mean? Poor girl.'

'I didn't quite catch the technical name. You know how she is. Loves the medical jargon. But I gathered it's the one that means you're afraid of crowds. I didn't want to show my ignorance by asking her to explain.'

James smiled to himself, as people do when they discover secrets, especially when the secret is that the other person is worse off. He felt too the encouraging warmth of affinity. At least they were both afraid of something. But what good was knowing this if they could never get together? As it was they were locked in separate cells, imprisoned by fear of people— his of himself, hers of others. If only they could get together they might help each other break out. Why not? And why not chance it? Could do no harm. Wouldn't matter if he made a fool of himself. Again.

Wouldn't be like making a fool of himself with people he had to go on seeing every day for ages afterwards. She'd be gone soon. And this time he'd try the head-on approach, nothing hidden, no pretending.

As soon as he could, he shut himself in his room and started writing.

Rosie,

The local grapevine (the woman who lives on the other side of you from us—my dad calls her the Beech Grove double agent) says you're staying with your uncle for a sort of holiday. It also says you suffer from a fear of crowds.

PLEASE DON'T STOP READING. I'd be angry as well if people went around telling other people what's the matter with me. Well, actually they do. That's one reason why I'm writing instead of coming round to talk to you or using the phone. PLEASE READ ON.

It might not be true that you can't stand crowds. If it isn't you'll be even more furious. I hope it isn't true, for your sake. But I'm supposing it is and that's why I'm writing.

I'll just come straight out with it, to save time. I suffer from chronic shyness. I'm all right with people I know well. And not so bad if I'm prepared for what's going to happen and what I'm going to say. When things are bad I also stammer. I'm worst of all with girls I like— if you understand me.

Mostly, people just tell me I'll grow out of it. I think my father decided years ago there's nothing really wrong with me except that I'm wet.

I'm telling you this for a couple of reasons. First of all, to explain why I acted like I did yesterday, in your garden, and today, on the phone. You probably thought I was stoned or a Neanderthal or something. Actually I was dumbstruck with shyness because I thought you looked so terrific. (Honest.)

The other reason is a bit more difficult to explain. I'll do the best I can.

Here I am, too shy to come and talk to you so I keep out of the way, when what I'd really like to do is get to know you. And there are you, in a strange place, all right about talking to one or two people at a time, but not able to go out because you can't stand crowds.

It seems to me that we both suffer from being scared in ways we can't control. I mean that's what gets to me the most—that I can't control being shy. It just sort of comes over me, like a wave, and drowns me, suffocates me, strangles me, so I can't say anything sensible, never mind what I want to say. And it makes me behave like someone with crossed wires.

I hate looking so stupid. I expect it's pretty much the same for you.

Well, I thought, if we could get together somehow, if you would like to, I mean, at least we'd have this in common. We'd understand each other. And maybe once I got over my shyness I'd be someone for you to talk to instead of being on your own all the time. Just let me know. Phone if you like so long as you don't mind me stammering back at you!

James Taggart.

That night, slipping out about eleven o'clock on the pretext of getting some fresh air before bed, and having ensured no one was around to catch him at it, he pushed his letter through the Bells' letterbox.

Next morning, just after his parents left for work, the telephone rang.

'This is Margot Bell.'

'Heh, heh, hello.'

'That must be James.'

'Yes.'

'It was you I wanted to talk to, James. Please don't

bother Rosie. I'm sure you were only being friendly. But she really isn't well. She's better on her own. That's why she came here. I hope you'll understand. Thank you, James. Mustn't keep you talking, I'm late for the office. Give my best to your parents.'

He took a hammer and butchered the tree house with satisfying violence.

When it was done, bruised and splintered spars of wood lying where he had dropped them around the foot of the tree, he climbed higher, to the topmost branch that would bear his weight, and sat there, swaying in the breeze, clinging on, almost enjoying this different fear for a change, a fear strong and fresh enough to override at last the crushing embarrassment of Mrs. Bell's call.

He'd been up this high only once before, the day his shyness took hold. He often thought of it, but now, clinging there in a sweat chilled by the breeze, he not only remembered it, but felt it again with as much clarity and pain as he had felt the first time.

When at last he was calm he climbed down and went inside.

Immediately, the phone rang.

'Rosie.'

He slammed the receiver down but wasn't out

of the room before it rang again. He let it yell in its maddening baby-demanding way till he could refuse no longer.

'Please don't hang up . . . This morning, my aunt, I'm sorry. I tried to stop her. She saw your note. I mean, she found it and brought it to me and wanted to know who it was from and what it said. I didn't tell her, only it was from you and you were offering to keep me company . . . She isn't awful, only trying to help . . . You don't have to say anything, I just wanted you to know I didn't . . . Well . . . Thanks anyway for telling me about yourself. I'm sorry you suffer like that, I wish I could help but . . . I liked getting your letter, though, just as a letter, I mean . . . We can't get together—not because of my aunt—something else . . . I can't explain . . . But I thought if you wanted to write again, well, I'd like that, and, I thought, in case of further interceptions, you could always post it to me in the tree in your garden. There's a kind of knothole just where the first branch hangs over the fence. You could put it in there and I'd pick it up when the coast was clear. I could phone you when I'd read it, if you like . . . That's all I wanted to say . . . I'll wait for a bit in case you want to say anything, then hang up . . .'

'OK. That's a, that's a, that's a good idea.'

'Great! I'll go now, then. Bye.'

Rosie,

Did you see I smashed up the tree house? I was mad with your aunt after her phone call and took it out on the tree house. Which is a pity in a way, because I used to love it. I used to sit up there for hours. Nobody else ever came up, nobody. It was my private place.

It had a lot to do with me being shy. After I'd smashed it up this morning, I climbed as high as I could and sat there like a crow looking down on our house and yours and the others all round, and remembering the first time I went up there.

It was the day after my eleventh birthday. In the yard at school a few of us were playing the kissing game. It was a kind of ritual. We were paired up with a girl by drawing lots. Then we went off, each pair in turn, behind the gym where nobody could see, and we had as long as it took the other kids to sing one of the songs from the top ten. We thought it was pretty hot stuff!

There was one girl I really liked. She was the first girl I ever fancied. And I thought she felt the same about me. I was desperate to kiss her. Before then, it had just been a game, and I hadn't been that keen on the bit behind the gym. But that day I drew lots for her.

While I waited for our turn I started shaking with excitement. And as soon as we were out of sight I tried my hardest to let her know how I felt about her. I thought I knew what you had to do, I'd seen it enough on TV and watching older people at it. But I hadn't had any proper practice. Not her, though. She really knew how! But really! I couldn't believe it. She took my breath away! By the time the song was finished and we had to join the others I could hardly stay on my feet I felt so weak with surprise and pleasure.

That afternoon I was in a daze. Neither my mind nor, much less, my body could untangle themselves from the glory of those few moments behind the gym. I'd never known anything like it! All I wanted was to be with her and doing it again. The world wasn't the same place any more.

Then I heard my name being called. The Head wanted to see me. In her office she glowered at me, accused me of foul deeds, of disgraceful acts. The girl had complained, she'd described in vivid detail, so the Head said, various filthy things I was supposed to have done. I denied it all. Denial not accepted. How could a nice, well-brought-up girl like her make up such things? (What about me? Wasn't I a nice well-brought-up boy? How would I know about them either?)

I tried to explain. Don't lie, she said. Did I want to make matters worse? Threatened to call my parents, fetch the police, expel me from the school. I broke down and wept, pleaded that I was innocent. She lectured me, asked what I thought would happen to the school's reputation never mind my own if such a thing as this got out.

Then she told me the girl had promised she would do nothing more about it so long as I promised to keep completely away from her, and never bother her again at school or anywhere else. If I did this, the Head said she would take things no further. But as punishment I would have to remain inside, under supervision, during all playtimes and dinnertimes for the rest of the term, my last before I went on to secondary school and was no longer, she was thankful to say, her responsibility. To put an end to the misery I agreed. I've hated myself for doing that ever since.

As I ran home, the girl was there, waiting, near my house. I ran past on the other side of the road. She stood and watched, laughing and singing the song they had sung during our turn at the kissing game.

I was so upset I couldn't go inside. I knew my mother would be there and I couldn't face her. I didn't know how to tell her what had happened. It was impossible. And I didn't know why the girl had behaved like she had. (Why would she? Can you explain it? I still don't understand.) So I ran into the garden and climbed the tree. Up and up to the topmost branches. The Beech Grove double agent saw me and raised the alarm. She and my mother tried to coax me down. I wouldn't. And I couldn't say anything. The words stuck in my throat.

Neighbours came out to look. My mother became more and more desperate. I could hear people telling her to fetch the fire brigade. Luckily before she did Dad came home. He persuaded everybody to leave. I thought he'd try and climb up to me. But he didn't. He left me where I was.

I stayed there till after dark. By then I had calmed down. In fact, a strange kind of steely control had come over me, like armour. I climbed down and went into the kitchen where my parents were sitting at the table with a half-finished meal in front of them.

I said, 'Could I have some corn, corn, cornflakes, please.'

That was all I wanted—cornflakes.

And that was the first time I stammered.

When I'd eaten, my father said, 'Got it out of your system, whatever it was?'

All I could do was nod. Nothing more was said and I went to bed.

Isn't that pathetic? All say Ah! You'd have thought I'd have got over it by now, grown out of it, like everybody tells me I should have done. It isn't as if I don't know why I'm shy and can't trust girls. I do know. But knowing doesn't seem to change anything. In a way it only makes it worse.

I thought I'd tell you.

James.

His letter took all day to write, drafting and redrafting. He planted it in the hole in the tree a few minutes before his mother arrived home.

At dinner his father said, 'I see the deed is done but the resulting mess isn't cleared up.'

'I'll do it tomorrow.'

'Can't have taken all day to demolish the thing. God knows how you spend your time at my expense.'

'Planning what I'll do when I take over the world.'

'You and all the other teenage layabouts, you mean.'

'Now, you two,' his mother said.

He dreamed that night of being at the top, the very top, only the sky above him, of his tree. But he was not alone. Rosie was with him. They were naked. He was her branch. She straddled him, face to face, clinging, and kissing him with a devouring passion.

Next morning he waited for an hour after his parents and (he was watching for them) the Bells had left for work. But the phone remained silent. Doubts began to flicker in his mind. He fled into the garden, where he distracted himself by gathering the broken tree house timber into a pyramid on a patch of untended ground at the bottom of the garden, adding whatever other flammable rubbish he could find. When it was done he returned to the house, needing newspaper and matches to light the bonfire. He was no sooner inside than the phone rang.

'Rosie.'

'You got it?'

'This morning. After they left . . . I don't know what to say.'

'You don't, don't have to, have to—'

'I know I don't have to say anything. But I want

to. I mean, you've told me all this about you. There's something I want to tell you about me.'

'. . . OK.'

'Not on the phone, though. It doesn't feel right. And there's something I want to give you as well.'

'How then?'

'You were making a bonfire. Are you going to light it?'

'Yes. I came in for, for matches.'

'I've been watching you. All the time. All yesterday. When you were sitting in the tree I looked at you through my uncle's binoculars. He bird-watches sometimes. I could see it all happening in your face. What you told me.'

They were silent. Only the sizzle of telephone static in his ear. He could hardly breathe.

'Go back into the garden. By the tree. Stand close to the fence there . . . OK?'

He could say nothing. She put the phone down.

He waited by the tree, leaning against the fence for ten, perhaps fifteen minutes. Had she meant it? Because he had not replied, had she thought he wouldn't come? But then he heard, close to his ear on the other side of the fence, the sound of breathing.

'James?' His name was hardly more than whispered.

'Yes?'

'You haven't lit your bonfire.'

'I thought I'd, I'd do it later. After . . .'

'I like bonfires. We used to roast potatoes in ours. Now it's barbecues with all the gear and that's not the same.'

'When I . . . start it, I'll row, roast one for you.'

'Thanks.'

They were silent.

'Your letter.'

'Yes?'

'What I wanted to tell you. It's not that I'm afraid of crowds. We just say that because it's easier. I can't talk about it usually. But . . . You see, the thing is, I was out one night a few months ago with a boyfriend. He swore he really liked me. Loved me, actually, he said . . . That word! What does it mean? . . . And wanted us—you know—to have sex. But I didn't want to, not yet, I wasn't ready . . . Anyway, on the way home we met some of his friends from work. He called them his mates. Don't you think it odd, James, that men call each other mates? I mean, isn't it a bit suspect? . . . Well, they weren't exactly drunk. Merry, I suppose people would call it. Game for anything they said . . . How people love games! Boys especially. They think they can get away with anything so long as they call it a game. And you're supposed to put up with it, and excuse them, whatever they do, girls have to at any rate, as if it wasn't real, didn't really happen, only pretending. I hate games and I don't pretend about anything anymore. There's only real, there's only what happens . . . Well, anyway, they played a sort of kissing game with me. Not that I had any choice. My so-called boyfriend was playing too. In fact, he was all for it. Having a great time, he was! Really enjoying himself. And it didn't stop at kissing. Kissing was only kids' stuff to them. They had lots more fun, knew lots more games than that. They even started competing to see who knew more than the others . . . No one sang a song while it happened and it lasted more than your few minutes behind the gym, James . . . A lifetime already.'

He could hear her heavy, urgent breathing now.

'Rosie?'

'Don't say anything, please don't say anything. There's nothing you can say that would help. Everybody's tried. It only makes it worse. But there's something you can do.'

'What?'

'Will you put your hand up so it's above the top of the fence?'

'Sure.'

He raised his right arm till his hand was clear of the fence and held it there, palm towards her. He watched, trembling with anticipation, as her slim, long-fingered left hand, appearing above the fence, reached up hesitantly, slowly, and at last with sudden decision laid itself palm to palm, fingers to fingers on his.

And then their fingers meshed and she gripped hard, locking their hands together.

She held him a moment, before saying, 'Can you stand so your head is above the fence?'

He glanced down. 'If we move a bit to, to your left.'

There the roots and bowl of the tree caused the ground to rise higher.

They edged along till their heads were visible.

From the second they could see each other her eyes held his eyes as firmly as her hand gripped his.

For some long time they gazed at each other, separated by only the thickness of the fence.

At last she said, 'When it was over, their kissing game, I made myself a promise. I can keep it now.'

'What?'

'Will you —'

'What?'

'Kiss me?'

'I wan, wanted to. Since I saw, saw, saw you.'

'Say it without stammering.'

He shook his head.

'You can. Say it!'

He took a deep breath. 'I wanted to since I saw you.'

'There, you see!' She laughed. 'I bet you imagined doing it?'

'Yes.'

'And more?'

He smiled.

'At night. In bed.'

'Yes. You too?'

'Oh yes, I've been imagining . . . So kiss me, why don't you?'

'Is that wha, what you wanted to give me?'

'And something else.'

'My lucky day!'

He inclined his head, leaned across the small distance that separated them till his lips touched hers, closed his eyes, instinctively raised his left hand, grasped her head, and pressed his mouth to hers, his whole body now straining against the fence.

Rosie found a gap in the fence, inserted the point of the carving knife into it, and with all her strength rammed the blade through at the level of her waist.

From her bedroom window, using her uncle's binoculars, she kept watch on the bonfire. The fiercest flames were dying now but thick grey-blue smoke still curled into the air, veiling the upper branches of the tree as the breeze caught it, thinned it out, and carried it away across the garden, swirling up into the sky.

Thrown Out

To the Environmental Services Officer

Dear Sir,

I live in a hut in the wood.

I built the hut with my own hands.

I only used materials I found in builders' skips and on rubbish dumps.

You wouldn't believe the stuff people throw away, most of it reusable with a bit of thought and work.

I made the frame of the hut out of lengths of two-by-four thrown out of a house being renovated.

I made the walls out of pieces of blockboard thrown out of a factory where they were putting up new partitions for offices.

I covered the outside of the walls with black PVC builders use for damp course lining before they pour concrete floors. They throw out the offcuts, but it's easy to nail them to the walls and overlap them like roof tiles, to keep the rain out.

I nailed some more blockboard to the frame to make the inside walls, which I painted various colours according to what I could find in leftover cans of paint.

For decoration I've pinned up pictures cut from magazines. There are plenty of those thrown out with people's household rubbish every week.

I get a lot of other things that way as well. Yesterday, for example, I found a whole precooked chicken still wrapped from the supermarket and within its use-by date. The day before, an unopened tin of sardines.

And food isn't all.

I've a nice bottle of shampoo, a quarter full, from last week. And a nice pair of trekker boots exactly my size. Fairly well used but plenty of life in them yet.

(You can always tell when there's a new fashion for something because you find the now out-of-fashion stuff thrown out, even quite new often. I collect that kind of thing and sell it at the weekly farmer's market in town. Brings in enough to keep me going for cash very nicely.)

For heating I use a thrown-out wood-burning stove, one of those black iron ones made to look old-fashioned. I made a chimney for it out of thrown-out metal drainpipes. I'm well supplied with wood to burn, of course, from fallen branches. I cut them up with a saw or an axe, both of which I bought secondhand. You do need good tools to live the way I do.

I use a thrown-out kettle for boiling water, a thrown-out saucepan for cooking veg, a thrown-out frying pan for fry-ups, and a thrown out roasting pan for doing meat.

Most of my food, in case you're wondering, I get for rock-bottom prices from shops in town just before closing time, especially on Saturdays, when they want to get rid of stock that won't keep till Monday. Some of the shopkeepers know me now and give the stuff to me for nothing. People are generous on the whole. That is, if you keep yourself clean and look reasonably presentable and behave well.

So how do I stay clean?

I've fixed up a gutter (thrown-out) along the edge of the roof, which drains into a thrown-out plastic drum. This provides rainwater for washing my clothes and myself in the ordinary way.

For a proper all-over wash I go to a sports club once a week, where I clean the changing rooms, lavatories and washrooms for the minimum rate of pay, and take a shower afterwards. That kills not two but three birds with one stone: a bit more income, a good wash, and they also have a washing machine, of course, so I do my week's laundry while I'm cleaning.

No one can say I'm dirty.

Inside my hut are the following:

My bed. A thrown-out single bedstead, a bit squeaky in the springs but who cares? There's nobody else to hear it but me.

A mattress I made myself out of thrown-out cloth stuffed with thrown-out polystyrene—the sort that looks like white puffed wheat. I used hay for a while, but you have to renew it quite often. There are plenty of thrown-out mattresses to be had but I don't fancy them. You never know who's slept on them or what diseases they had. I'm very careful when it comes to that sort of thing. And I don't like mucky things.

By now I needn't tell you that the sheets and blankets I use were thrown out. They're OK because I inspected them carefully for any nasty stains and gave them a couple of good washes in the sports club washing machine before using them.

A stripped, pinewood table two meters by one and a half, suitable for seating four to a meal, if I ever had guests, thrown out of a house they were renovating in a different style. I also use this as my desk.

I picked up a little stripped wood bedside cabinet from the same place.

Two chairs. A thrown out armchair—you know the sort, with wings and little wooden legs that you see in old people's homes. In fact, this one came from a house where an old person had died and they were throwing out the furniture they didn't want. I gave it a good clean with thrown-out furniture shampoo and dried it in the sun. It came up beautifully, and I don't care if it does look a bit old people's homey. It's comfortable.

The other chair is a Windsor dining chair with a couple of the rods missing from the back, but it's firm enough and does well. I've sanded it down so that it has the stripped wood look of the table.

I bought a loose cover from a charity shop to put over the armchair because the design of the upholstery is big flowers and curly leaves, which, to be honest, isn't my taste and I wanted something that was. The loose cover is a golden yellow like the sun in the late afternoon.

A nest of shelves I made of thrown-out storage boxes open at the front. I keep my books—sixteen of them—in one compartment, pans in another, personal bits and pieces in another, my crocks in another (thrown-out plates, soup bowl, mugs, glasses, knives, forks, spoons, cooking gear).

A thrown-out wind-up radio.

Ditto clock.

Ditto some battery powered lamps. (It's not easy to find thrown-out batteries that work, so I have to buy them.)

An oil lamp (again, oil has to be bought).

Candles (also bought, and as a last resort, though I do like the light they give, but it isn't good to read by). Anyway, I tend to go to bed when it's dark and get up with the sun.

You'll probably say that there is a danger of causing a fire that could burn down not only my hut but also set fire to the wood. I can only reply that I am very careful, and have bought a fire extinguisher, just in case.

What haven't I mentioned that you want to know about?

Oh yes, the lav. I used to go in the wood, but it's a bit of a palaver and you don't want to use the same place every time. I dug a pit once for regular use, but it soon starts to smell and you need disinfectant, which makes it smell even worse. So now I have a chemical toilet I was given as payment by a man who was refurbishing his camper. I did a bit of work for him, lifting and carrying. (He was going to throw it out, so it wasn't much of a payment so far as he was concerned.) I empty it once a week. This is the worst job and I'm trying to think of how to make it easier.

You asked me why I'm living in my hut.

There are two reasons.

First, because I'm fed up with the human race and the way it goes on. Wars, money money money, rat race jobs, mortgages, celebrity crap, dodgy politicians, and half the world or more starving while the other half or less (us) throw out enough stuff to make life OK for the starving half.

The second reason is I don't want to do anything. They say you have to do something with your life.

They mean busy busy busy. Ambition. Getting rich. Having families. Doing doing doing.

But why?

What makes it better doing things than doing nothing?

If people want to do do do, I don't mind.

Though I do mind about a lot of what they do, because I think it is wrong.

So why should anybody care that I am doing nothing? I'm not bothering them. I'm not asking them for anything. I don't steal from them. I don't con them out of money or goods. I don't interfere with their lives in any way. I only take what they have thrown out. And I make use of it.

What's wrong with that?

In fact, isn't it good?

You ask what I do all day.

I listen to the wind in the trees.

I listen to the birds singing.

I watch the animals that come by my hut. You'd be surprised how many there are.

I cook my food and enjoy eating it in my hut or outside, where I'm making a little garden to grow things. I have lettuce growing there already and potatoes and I've planted a few cabbages. I have plans for more. I get the plants from the garden centre when they throw them out because they aren't selling or are a bit off. I lose some, but if you care for them properly it's surprising how many pick up and grow well.

I listen to the radio for music and news, and I like the plays they put on sometimes.

And I am learning new skills all the time: How to make things. How to take care of myself and my environment.

What I am learning most about is myself. It is not as easy to live on your own as people might think it is.

I am learning to be independent and to stand on my own two feet, without sponging off anyone.

Of course, I would like to live with someone who would like to live the way I do.

I have faith this will happen.

Sometimes people say that I have double standards. Even that I am a hypocrite, because I use things other people have made.

But the stuff has been made, there's nothing I can do about that. And it has been thrown out, so I'm making use of it when it would only add to the mountain of so-called rubbish we bury and burn and throw into the sea every day.

You could say my occupation is recycling rubbish.

And I know from the labels that a lot of the stuff is made in places like China where the workers are virtually slaves. That is wrong also.

I read a lot. Books are thrown away all the time, so there's plenty to choose from.

And I have a ticket for the local library, which is one of my best possessions. I can read there in comfort. I can use the Internet (it's there, so why not?). The staff are brilliant. They help me get the books I want.

I'm studying the history and ecology of our country, and am learning the names and types of every tree and flower, every bush and plant in the wood.

What am I doing?

I am living. That's what I'm doing.

I am happy living as I live.

But you have sent me this letter that says you are going to throw me out of my hut because it doesn't have planning permission.

And that you are going to pull my hut down — and throw it away as well, I suppose.

Why do you want to do that?

Just because some impersonal law says so?

Or because you don't like the way I live?

Why are you doing this?

That is what I'd like to know.

I am appealing to you, and to whoever gives you your orders, to let me stay where I am, doing nothing that bothers anybody and doing no harm.

Please leave me alone.

Please let me live my life in the way I want to.

From the Environmental Services Officer
Request refused on legal grounds.

Toska

A FRIEND GAVE ME THIS BOOK TO READ.

It's called *Happy Moscow.*

It's a Russian novel by someone called Andrey Platanov.

The stuff about him at the back of the book says he died in 1951.

This is not my kind of book usually. Russian books have all those unsayable names in them. I tried a book that's supposed to be a Big Best Classic. It was called *The Brothers Karamazov.*

No way. Couldn't do with it, Big Best Classic or not.

But you know how it is with friends.

You have to go along with them when they are keen about something.

And my friend Pauline was mad about this book *Happy Moscow*, so naturally I read it.

It starts with the girl called Moscow.

Reminds me of people like the Beckhams who call their children by the names of the places where they were conceived.

Just as well none of them was conceived in places like Pity Me, where my grandmother lived. (Hello, Pity Me, how you doing?) Or Dripping Springs, Texas. (Hi, Dripping Springs. Nice weather today.) Mind you, there was a girl in my infant school called Cherry Orchard. Can you imagine? Parents!

But back to Moscow.

She lived at the time of the Russian Revolution.

I had to look that up on Google. 1917 apparently. (I'm rubbish at history as well as at Russian names in books.)

Anyway, the point is, I learned a new word from Moscow's book.

Toskà.

I like learning interesting new words, don't you?

Toskà is a good one.

At the beginning of Moscow's book it says (I quote):

'No single word in English renders all the shades of *toskà*. At its deepest and most painful, it is a sensation of great spiritual anguish, often without specific cause. At less morbid levels it is a dull ache of the soul, a longing with nothing to long for, a sick pining, a vague restlessness, mental throes, yearning.

In particular cases it may be the desire for somebody or something specific, nostalgia, lovesickness. At the lowest level it grades into ennui, boredom.'

It says this is what a writer called Vladimir Nabokov says *toskà* means.

I don't know why Moscow couldn't have said that herself.

Well, no, I do. I'm like that with essays for school. I can always find what I want to say said better by someone else. And it is easier to write down what they say than try to say it all again in my own words, which are never as good. But I am always being told off for doing this. 'I want it in your own words,' they say. *They* being teachers of course. Ridiculous.

Anyhow, back to Moscow's quote.

Nearly all of this is how I feel right now.

Not bored.

But aching somewhere deep inside. Would that be in my soul? I have not considered my soul so far. Whether I have one or not. Or, rather, what I mean is, whether there is such a thing as a soul. Whether anyone has one.

Still, I do have an ache deep inside me, a pining, a vague restless yearning.

But for what?

Well, to start with for Henry James Benson.

I have indicated to this member of the male sex

as best I can without giving myself away completely what I feel about him. But no response. So far.

I suppose I could go as far as to say I am lovesick for him.

But apart from Henry James Benson, I do have to admit that there are times, quite often these days, when I suffer from a vague restlessness, when I wander about the house wanting something but not knowing what it is I want.

Growing pains, is what my grandfather calls this.

Teenage angst is what my father calls it.

Normal is what my mother calls it.

All of them say I will grow out of it, get over it, finito, done and dusted when I 'grow up'.

I detest the words 'grow up'.

'Why don't you grow up!' one or all of the aforementioned relatives snap at me when I am in my worst state of anguish, longing, pining, yearning, restlessness—see above.

Well, excuse me!

Now I have a word for it.

Now I can say, 'Oh, it's only my *toskà* on the go. Just live with it. I have to.'

Mind you, I also have to admit, that there is something enjoyable about being *toskà*.

Toskà can be a painful pleasure.

And to go by *Happy Moscow* and the bits of *The*

Brothers Karamazov I managed to read before dying of boredom, not to mention a couple of Russian short stories by someone called Chekhov that our teacher read to us, I would hazard a guess that being in a major state of *toskà and enjoying it for all it's worth* is pretty much the way all Russians are.

Though one ought not to make generalisations of this kind and be so judgemental.

So I'm told.

But to continue:

The storyteller of *Happy Moscow* says the name Moscow means 'honest'.

In the first chapter Moscow writes (I quote):

'Story by a girl with no Father or Mother about her Future Life: We are being taught to have minds, but minds are in heads, there is nothing on the outside. We must labour to live truthfully, I want to live the future life, I want there to be biscuits and jam and sweets and always to be able to walk by the trees in the fields. Otherwise I won't live, I won't feel like it. I want to live normally with happiness. There's nothing to say in addition.'

Already I feel Moscow is my friend. I have a mother and a father and sometimes wish I hadn't. (Not really. Only when I'm in a really bad *toskà*.)

And Moscow wants what I want.

To live normally and with happiness.

And like her, my aim is always to be honest.

With myself anyway.

And with other people as much as I can, however hard it is to be honest with them sometimes.

I want never to pretend or to lie about myself and about what happens and what I do—and don't do (which is sometimes as hard as doing something).

I do not want to pretend that what happens to me is anything else but what it *is*—what it feels like and what I think about it.

I want this, however much it may make me suffer from *toskà*.

Because it is impossible to translate *toskà* by one or two or even three English words, and because what it means is so deep and important in my own life, and I think in everyone's life, I shall use *toskà* whenever I mean all those things that the writer Nabokov says it means in Russian.

Toskà. Welcome to the English language.

And because we do not have those accent marks above letters in English I shall write it like this: *toska*.

I feel much better for having a name for what I feel right now.

Or rather, what I was feeling just now.

I feel better for having the name, the way you feel better when you are ill and you don't know why, and the doctor tells you the name for what is the matter with you.

Once you know the name of your ailment it seems to have no power over you any more.

Instead, you have power over it.

And power over yourself.

So thank you, Moscow the honest.

And thank you, Russia, for your Russian name for what I was feeling.

And a happy *toska* to you, one and all.

The end.

Like Life

BRAD AND EVE, BOTH SEVENTEEN, SIT ON A *park bench eating a cheeseburger in the afternoon sun.*

Eve: Something keeps bothering me.

Brad: There's always something bothering you. I've never known anybody so bothered.

Eve: How many people do you know?

Brad: Never counted them.

Eve: Not much to go on, then.

Brad: No, I'll give you that.

Eve: Well, anyway, something keeps bothering me.

Brad: What?

Eve: That I haven't done nothing yet.

Brad: Nothing like what?

Eve: Like life.

Brad: Like how like life?

Eve: Nothing like serious.

Brad: Serious? Serious like what?

Eve: Like something important.

Brad: You mean, I'm not important to you?

Eve: No. I mean yes, you are. But serious like in *serious*.

Brad: Serious like in *serious* how?

Eve: Like I mean serious like I haven't never really suffered or gone hungry or been really ill or been really *really* hurt.

Brad: It can be arranged.

Eve: Haven't really had any life.

Brad: What sort of life?

Eve: Like people you see on telly always with love troubles. Or like in wars or big disasters, like that soon-army what drowned people, where was it, in those islands somewhere. Or even people we know.

Brad: Like who?

Eve: Like Sam Briggs.

Brad: The boy that had the heart op and his mum died of a heart attack on the same day?

Eve: Like him. When I think about him I feel about like two years old.

Brad: Like a baby.

Eve: Like innocent. Or like I haven't been born yet. I don't hardly know what life's about yet, what it's *really* like.

Brad: Don't complain.

Eve: I'm not complaining.

Brad: It could happen yet.

Eve: I'm just describing.

Brad: Matter of fact, there is something, now you mention it.

Eve: Mention what?

Brad: Like life you want to happen to you.

Eve: So?

Brad: Well, you remember Karen.

Eve: In McDonald's the other night?

Brad: After *Sex in the City*. Her. Yes, her.

Eve: What about her?

Brad: She's got herself knocked up.

Eve: No!

Brad: Yes.

Eve: In the club?

Brad: Pregnant.

Eve: Well, she always was a bit of a tart.

Brad: Wouldn't say that.

Eve: How d'you know?

Brad: Saw her last night, didn't I.

Eve: I thought you was at the game?

Brad: I was.

Eve: And she was there?

Brad: She comes sometimes.

Eve: You never said.

Brad: You didn't ask.

Eve: So did she tell you who?

Brad: She did, yes.

(Pause)

Eve: Well, come on. Spit it out.

Brad: You really want to know?

Eve: Course I want to know, idiot!

Brad: Me.

Eve: You?

Brad: Yeah.

Eve: *You!*

Brad: Bit of an accident really.

Eve: Accident!

Brad: Yeah.

Eve: *Accident!*

Brad: Didn't mean to knock her up, did I!

Eve: What was you doing with her at all?

Brad: Well, like you said.

Eve: Like I said what?

Brad: That's life.

Sanctuary

THE ONLY WAY TO SAVE HIMSELF WAS TO *get inside.*

He'd be all right as soon as he was off the street.

Luckily, there was a café right there with a few tables free.

He made straight for the toilet where he locked himself in a cubicle and sat there till he'd calmed down. Then he washed his face in cold water and flicked his hair into shape—it was windy outside. He felt better, in control of himself, but was worried about going out onto the street in case he was attacked again.

The café wasn't busy, too early in the morning, between breakfast-time customers and mid-morning office workers and shoppers having their coffee break. He ordered a green tea, because that was his comfort drink at home when he felt upset, and a muffin because he felt he ought to order something more than a drink.

He sat at a table by the window, thinking that if he looked out at the street while he drank his tea he'd be able to familiarise himself with it and feel more confident when he went outside again. It was the strangeness of places that brought on the panic. But he never knew which places or when.

The winter day was damp and cold as well as windy. People hugged into their clothes and hurried past. He, a country boy, thought of them as cattle in a strop.

A girl walked by, eighteen or nineteen perhaps, his own age. But not hurrying like everyone else, nor as huddled up. She was wearing a kind of duffle coat with the hood up, her hands in the pockets. She glanced into the shop and caught his eye. They exchanged that kind of brief but intense look strangers give each other when there's an instant recognition or physical attraction or need.

When she'd gone out of view he wondered what it was about her that had caught him. He felt it in the pit of his stomach and between his legs.

A man came to the window and looked in. Then turned in the direction the girl had gone and gave a 'come here' wave.

He took a drink of tea, and when he looked again the girl was standing beside the man, peering into the shop, not at him but at the few other people and the two young women serving behind the counter.

The man was big, strongly built, well dressed like an office manager. Posh tan overcoat, red scarf, black trilby. He said a few words to the girl, handed her something, and walked away.

After a moment the girl came in and went to the counter. He wanted to watch and see what she bought, but thought it rude, so kept his eyes on the street.

He'd almost finished his tea, hadn't touched the muffin, he never wanted to eat after an attack. He wondered whether he should buy another tea, he didn't want it, but didn't feel ready to tackle the outside either. He hadn't decided when the girl came to his table and asked if he'd mind if she sat there. She had a foreign accent, he didn't know what, but quite liked it, it made him smile.

He said, no it was OK.

She put her mug of espresso on the table, undid her coat and sat opposite him. She had very black hair, shoulder length and a bit wavy. Her face was round and pale with big blue eyes and a straight nose, and a wide mouth with lips he thought very kissable. Under her coat she was slim and wearing a tight white high-necked top that showed her breasts and the nipples.

He tried not to stare at her. But his eyes kept sliding back for another look. She was watching him all the time.

After a couple of sips of coffee she said, 'I'm Nadia.'

'Jack,' he said. 'Hi.'

She nodded and smiled and took another sip of coffee.

'You looked a bit lonely,' she said. 'I thought you might like some company.'

'No, it's not that,' he said.

She watched him but didn't respond.

'On my way for an interview,' he said, unable to sit there saying nothing.

'A job?' she said. 'What sort?'

'No, not a job. Interview for a place at the uni,' he said, and added, thinking she might not understand, 'the university.'

'Clever!' she said but not mocking. 'To study?'

'Microbiology.'

'I don't know that.'

'Neither do I much.'

'What is it?'

'The study of very small bugs and things you can only see with a powerful microscope, and their effects on people.'

'Like, you mean, diseases?'

'Diseases and behaviour.'

She drank more coffee.

'You want your bun perhaps?' she said.

'My muffin? No.' Then realised why she'd asked. 'Would you like it?'

He pushed the plate towards her. She took the muffin, stripped off its paper cup and began to eat quite hungrily.

She looked at him apologetically, and said, 'No breakfast.'

They sat in silence till she finished eating, dabbing up fallen crumbs and bits off the paper cup with her fingertip and licking them off.

He couldn't take his eyes from her now.

'On your way to work?' he asked.

'Work? No. When is your interview?'

'This afternoon. At two.'

'A long wait.'

'Didn't want to be late, and the trains from home aren't that frequent.'

'You don't live here?'

'No. Wiltshire.'

'Wilt-shire,' she said, smiling and pronouncing each syllable.

'Thought of spending some time at the British Museum but—well—'

She waited, expecting him to go on. When he didn't, but instead looked out at the street, she said, 'Well?'

He gave her a nervous look. He didn't like talking about it. People didn't understand, thought he was just being weak-willed. But he remembered that look of instant recognition and there was something about her that made him want to tell her.

'Well, the thing is, I suffer from agoraphobia.'

'Agora?'

'Agoraphobia. Fear of open spaces. Not always everywhere. But I never know where.'

'And what happens?'

'I kind of go to pieces. Can't make sense of anything. Signs for instance. I panic and can't get my breath. My body goes weak and if I'm not careful I collapse.'

'So what you do?'

'Get inside.'

'It happen this morning?'

'Just outside. That's why I came in.'

'Nasty.'

'Not nice, that's true.'

'But why no one with you?'

'My parents offered. And a teacher. But I wanted to do it on my own. I mean, if I'm given a place here I'll have to move about on my own. We did a dry run, my father and me, a week ago, so I'd know where to go and how to get there. I thought I'd be OK. But I just lost it this morning. I guess the nerves about the interview brought it on.'

'So what you do now?'

'Try again, what else?'

She gave him a thoughtful look.

He smiled and shrugged.

'If you like,' she said after a moment, 'you come to my place. Wait there. Then I walk you where you have to go.'

'Really?'

'I know what it's like. On your own in strange place.'

'You're not British?'

'Ukrainian. Came to study English. But have to work because of money.'

'It's very good, your English.'

'My passion at school. And better living here.'

'How long?'

'Here? One year.'

She drained her mug, looked at him, smiling, and said, 'So, you come to my place?'

He couldn't resist even had he wanted to.

It was a small room in a house of one-room flats not far from the station. A table, a dining chair, a battered armchair, a cheap wardrobe, and a double bed with a gaudy cover. There was a bedside cabinet with a lamp on it of a naked woman with an arm raised above her head that was supposed to hold a bulb but didn't. A little kitchen area was partitioned off from the bedroom with a weary, faded curtain over the doorway, and through another open door a small bathroom with only a shower, hand basin and loo. The room had a single window, curtained with tired muslin and heavy blue drapes hanging at the sides. His mother would have said the curtains could do with a good wash and the window as well. But otherwise the room was bare. Empty. No personal things. Nothing like his sister's room. No clothes, no makeup, no posters, no CDs, no books, no computer, not even a TV or radio. A room belonging to nobody.

He didn't quite know what to do or where to put himself.

'Sit,' she said, taking off her coat and hanging it behind the door, and taking his and hanging it over hers.

'You'd like coffee?' she asked. 'Tea? Something?'

He sat at the table. 'I'm OK, thanks.'

She sat on the edge of the bed, arms stretched to her sides, her hands supporting her. Long legs in tight blue jeans and her tight white top and pale face, and big eyes and black hair in waves.

They looked at each other, he unsure now and she as if waiting for something to happen, something to be said, he didn't know what, which made him even more uncomfortable. He began to wonder if he should have come here and whether he should go.

Then she took a deep breath and said, 'Look. Sorry.

I lied. Well, no, not lie. I *am* Ukrainian. I *did* think I was to study English. That's what they said, the people who brought me. The men. They said they fix everything. Passport. Visa. Everything. And somewhere to live. I work part-time for them as secretary and study part-time. I was very eager, you know. It was my dream. Come to England. Study language. The men seemed honest. They seemed kind. They want money to get me here and set up. A lot of money. But I save from a job, and my aunt, my favourite in our family and I am hers, I told her about plan, she gave me rest of money. So I paid and everything fixed. But it wasn't what I expect. None of it. The men who brought me not the men who fixed it. They shut me in room with five other girls from different places. Romania, Bulgaria, Russia. We not allowed out. Never. They keep us in that room for many days. They told us we work for them to pay off money they say we owe. They say they show us the work we do. And it began with—it began with—'

She was crying now. Tears but no sounds. Only the words she was speaking like a recorded voice machine.

He didn't know what to do, sat fixed in his chair.

'The men, three of them. They took us. Each of the girls. You know? Used us. It was not my first time. I had boy at home. But it was—'

The crying stopped her talking. But still no other sounds. No sobs, no gasping for breath, no wracked movements. She was rock still. Only tears and a raw blank look.

He had never seen anything so upsetting. Tears came to his eyes. He struggled not to break down.

There was silence for a long time.

Then she sniffed, wiped her eyes and began again.

'They make me work from here. One of them is boss. He brings me from place where they keep us. He brings me in van with no windows so I can't see where we go. One of his men watches all day what I do and stop me running away. They take me back in van when I've done enough. Sometimes it is all night as well as all day. The boss makes me pick up men and bring them here. He takes all money. He tells me what to charge. If I don't give him right amount afterwards he beats me. When he feels like it he has me himself. Mostly, it's his man who's with me. But the boss with me this morning. You saw him?'

He nodded, unable to speak.

'He saw me look at you. He's clever. Misses nothing. He told me to pick you up. And here you are.'

She stirred. Got up and went to the bathroom. Blew her nose. Drank some water. Came back. Sat down again.

'I lie. Sorry.'

'I don't want —' he said.

'No. I saw you sitting in the café. You look lonely. Worried also. I can't help looking at you. It wasn't I thought you'd be a good trick. Lonely men are. Older men especially. The boss tell look for the lonely ones, the ones who need company, need help, want relief. They're the easiest. But not what I thought about you. When I see you I think about myself. You look like I feel all the time. I say to him you weren't for me. But he say I have to. He say you'd be easy.'

'He was right.'

She tried to smile. It was enough to lighten her eyes. 'Yes! You must be more careful. It's dangerous out there!'

He took a deep breath and let it out. He looked at her and knew he wanted her. But not like this. Not as one of the men she was forced to go with. And not here where she had to do what they wanted. But he did want her. He'd never had a girl. She'd be his first. At his age, at eighteen, he was so ashamed of this he lied when asked. Yes, he always said, yes, he'd had a few. He wouldn't give details, pretending to be shy about it.

He said, 'If I go without giving you any money, what will he do?'

'Beat me. He knows how without leaving ugly marks or breaking anything.'

The thought tightened his chest.

'I've got some money,' he said. 'I don't know if it's enough, but you can have it. How much do you need?'

'Depends what I've done for you.'

'Well, what's the cheapest?'

'No. I shouldn't have done this. I should have say you say no. But there was this something. Something. About you. I want to be with you.'

'But did you think I'd . . . have it with you?'

'You're angry.'

'I'm not angry. I'm puzzled.'

'I think nothing. Doing what I do, you stop thinking. You can't afford thinking. You cut your mind off. Cut your feelings off. Go dead inside. Do what you're told. Do what you have to. No thinking. Just wanting. Wanting someone to be with and not *do* any of that. Someone who want to be with me only because I'm me. That look you give me, it kind of wake me up. I *feel* it. Here.' She pointed to her stomach. 'I feel it here. But I don't come for you, not if he had not made me. The way I look at you give me away. They allow no feeling for anybody else. They want you not to be human. They want you to be machine for sex. All most of the men want.'

'But if I don't give you money, what are you going to do?'

'I be nice to him. I know what he likes. But I prefer he beat me than please him. I'm used to it.'

'Haven't you tried to escape?'

'I see what they do to girls who try. They make us watch. And I have no passport, no identity card, no work permit, no money, nothing. They take everything. Even clothes. Even things I brought with me. Personal things. What I do, even if I escape? Where I go?'

'There must be something you can do.'

'You no idea. Eh? No? No idea what the world is like for someone like me.'

'But can't I help? What can I do? I'd like to help.'

They looked at each other, he leaning towards her, urgent, she wary, assessing him.

And after a moment she said quietly, leaning towards him, as if she might be overheard, 'Something.'

He said as quietly, 'Tell me.'

'They not let us shop. We tell them what we want. They buy, if they say OK. Some things they won't.'

'What? What is it you want?'

'A crucifix.'

'A crucifix?'

'Like people wear round necks.'

'A cross, you mean? Or one with Christ on it?'

'A cross. A gold cross. Little. Easy to hide.'

He sat back.

She sighed, as if something long pent up had at last been let out.

'You're a Christian?' he asked.

'And also a Bible. They take mine. My cross and my Bible. They say only fools believe in God. They say the Bible is book of lies.'

'And you want me to buy them for you.'

'You are Christian?'

'Not especially.'

'You believe in God?'

'No. And I don't see how you can after what's happened.'

She looked hard at him. 'Do not blame God for what people do.'

'I don't, because I don't believe there's a God to blame. And if I were made to do what you're made to do I wouldn't survive. I wouldn't want to. I don't know how you live through it.'

She stood up, eased herself, and sat down on the bed again cross-legged.

'I tell you, I do not think when with a man. I do not think what he is doing or what he is making me do. What I do, I pray. From the minute I pick him up to the time he goes, I think of God. I give myself to God, not the man. This how I survive. So do not mock my belief.'

'I don't. I wasn't. I'm only saying I don't believe in God. In any god.'

'Because you do not have to. You have easy life. You never have to survive. You do not know the word. What it means. Only people who will die know what survive means.'

He felt humbled. A child compared with this girl sitting on an ugly bed in this nobody-room where she suffered torture every day.

'My faith and prayers keep me alive,' she went on. 'A cross and a Bible help.'

'Won't they take them from you?'

'I hide them here. Then smuggle them where they keep us and hide them there. I know of places. Will you do it? Will you buy them for me?'

'You mean now?'

'You have time. And money. They cost not much. Less than you pay for me. Even the cheapest.'

He knew he'd do it.

'But if someone is watching all the time, won't he see me leave and come to get the money?'

'I tell him you want more than you have and go to get money. He see you come back and it will be OK.'

He got up and put his coat on.

'I'll do it. The only thing is —'

'Ah, yes! Your agora.'

'Yes.'

'Listen. A jeweller shop. Not far. Turn left from this building. On same side. A bookshop farther along. They have a little Bible? Not far. Not long. Maybe the agora not happen.'

He had no trouble. Not a twinge of his phobia. Instead a fearful excitement he'd never felt before that made his heart beat faster and his body move more quickly. He bought a little gold cross on a thin silver chain. The Bible was as small as a paperback, printed on very thin paper. He put them in his pockets so the man on the watch wouldn't see he was carrying anything. And he stopped at a cash dispenser and withdrew money to give to her.

On the way back he saw an alley he'd noticed on the way to the shops. It ran down the side of the building next to the flats. He wondered if it led to the back of them. On the spur of the moment he dodged into the alley. It did lead to the rear of her building. And there was a service door, as he'd hoped there would be.

He made his way to the stairs. Her room was on the third floor. The stairs were dingy, covered in worn carpet, the lights had to be on even in daytime. The windows at the head of the stairs on each floor were so grimy he couldn't see through them.

When he reached her door he paused, listening, his ear close.

Nothing. No voices. No sound of movement.

He tapped quietly with his fingertips.

The door opened instantly, but instead of the girl there was a man. Very big, thickset, shaven bullish head, a face like carved rock and eyes as brutal as his body.

Before he could say or do anything the man grabbed his arm, pulled him into the room, kicked the door shut, and held him from behind in an armlock so painful he cried out.

The girl was wedged in the corner behind the table, her arms hugging herself in fear.

Nothing was said. While holding him with one hand the man began turning out his pockets. His wallet, book for reading on the train, pen, letter from the university, the folded street map he'd Googled of the area between the station and the place for the interview, his mobile, the money he'd just withdrawn from the dispenser. And the Bible and the cross on its chain. All thrown like litter onto the bed.

When the man was sure he had found everything he picked up the Bible and the cross and held them in front of Jack's face.

'What's this, then?'

'Mine,' he said.

The twist the man gave his arm caused another yell of pain.

'You just bought them. I saw you. They're for her, aren't they! She told me.'

Another twist, another yell. Followed by a turning throw that landed him on his back on the floor.

'Not a good notion, sonny. Not a good idea.'

The man stamped down hard on his stomach. Another bellow of pain and he was fighting for breath.

But before he could recover, the man dragged him to his feet and threw him against the wall between the door and the wardrobe. His head came down to meet his knees as he gasped for breath, but as he bent, the man hit his forehead with a sledgehammer fist, which knocked him upright and banged his head against the wall. The blow dazed him. The pain weakened him so much his legs gave way and he slithered to the ground, panting, slavering bile.

The man was preparing another assault when a hard crack exploded on his head.

The man buckled, sagged, and collapsed.

The girl was standing over him with the remains of the bedside lamp in her hands.

No one moved.

The man lay facedown. The naked woman's raised arm was impaled in the back of his head. The rest of her body, broken off at the knees, rose into the air as if she had dived into the man's skull. Blood was running down his neck onto the floor.

Jack was the first to regain his senses. He pushed himself to his feet, went to the girl and eased the base of the lamp from her hands. Still she didn't move or take her eyes off the man.

'We've got to go,' he said. 'We've got to get away from here.'

No response.

He threw the remains of the lamp onto the bed and, taking her by the shoulders, turned her to face him.

'Nadia,' he said, 'Nadia, listen. We've got to get out of here.'

Still nothing. A blank stare.

He picked the cross and the Bible from where they had fallen on the floor, his wallet and mobile, and the money from the bed and stuffed them into his pockets. He fetched Nadia's coat from behind the door and held it in front of her.

'Nadia,' he said firmly, 'put your coat on.'

It took a long moment for the instruction to seep in. But slowly, robot-like, she turned and like a child allowed him to put her coat on for her.

He turned her to face him again and buttoned the coat.

'Is there anything of yours in the room?' he asked. 'Anything personal? Anything *yours*?'

Again his words took an age to sink in. But then her eyes came back to life. She looked round as if seeing the place for the first time, and shook her head.

'Nothing,' he said. 'You're sure?'

She nodded.

'Come on, then. We have to go. *Now.*'

He took her hand and, pulling her after him, rushed out of the room, down the stairs and out of the service door at the back of the flats.

Here he paused, holding her by both arms, facing him.

'We must get away from here. We're going to the station. We'll think what to do when we get there. OK, Nadia? . . . OK?'

She nodded, her eyes full of fear, her body stiff and trembling.

'We have to look normal,' he said. 'Don't rush. Just walk. OK?'

She nodded again.

He took her hand and led her to the alley.

In the station forecourt he made straight for one of the cafés and sat her at a table inside and out of view of the door, then ordered tea for them both into which he poured an overdose of sugar. He realised they were in shock and knew from First Aid classes at school how hot sweet tea was good for that.

He had to persuade her to drink. She was still unable to say anything, as if her breath was locked up, and reacted slowly to anything he said. Her hand was cold and damp.

Now he began to shiver and broke into a cold sweat as well.

Delayed reaction, he told himself. He'd felt it before whenever he'd suffered an agora attack.

Keep a grip, he thought. I've got to keep a grip. Breathe slowly, make yourself relax from the feet up. Don't let it get a hold on you.

He took a deep breath and let it out slowly. Made his body go slack.

I have to decide what to do, he thought. The man's dead, that's for sure. Someone, the boss, another thug, will come looking. They'll find the body. But what will they do? Call the police. But would they? The girl's an illegal immigrant they smuggled into the country. They're using her in an illegal business. Not just using her, abusing her. And the other girls. It's a racket, a criminal business. If they call the police they've had it. The police will arrest them and close them down. The last thing they want is the police to get involved. So what will they do? Get rid of the body. Clear up the mess.

Keep it to themselves. But they'll know the girl has gone. They won't like that. They'll look for her. If she went to the police, they'd have had it. If she's trying to escape, the nearest station is one place they'll look pretty quick.

So they mustn't stay here. But where could they go? He knew no one in the city. A hotel? He wouldn't know how to handle checking in and it would be too risky anyway. He couldn't afford it. They couldn't stay for longer than a day. And what about his parents? He'd have to phone them. What would he tell them?

He finished his tea. Made Nadia finish hers.

She leaned to him with frightened eyes.

'He is dead?'

He nodded and squeezed her hand.

'I think so.'

'I kill him,' she said.

She began to cry. He handed her a paper napkin from the container on the table. She wiped her eyes, blew her nose, and said, 'I wish to go home.'

And suddenly he knew there was only one thing they could do.

'Listen, Nadia. We've got to get away from here. They'll be looking for you. You'll have to come with me. We'll catch the first train that gets us on the way home, to my home, to where I live. You'll be safe there. I'm going to buy a ticket for you. Can you wait here while I do that? They won't know me, but they do know you. So you have to stay out of sight. OK? Understand? Can you do that?'

She shivered as he asked, but said yes she could do that.

'You mustn't move. OK? Promise?'

'Yes,' she said.

It was only then he remembered the cross and Bible. He took them from his pocket and handed them to her. She gave a little cry of relief, took them, put the Bible on the table in front of her, unhooked the chain of the cross and hung it round her neck, before opening the Bible and gazing at the pages, turning them over, as if she had recovered an old friend thought to be lost.

He went to the ticket office.

When he got back she was still there but looking terrified, deathly pale and wild eyed and gripping the Bible in her hands.

He'd checked the train departures. There was one in ten minutes that would get them halfway. They'd have more than an hour to wait for their connection, but they'd be a long way from the city and safe.

'Come,' he said.

She jumped up, no longer sluggish now but overanxious, wanting to run, wanting to flee.

He found them seats on the side away from the platform. He sat her by the window, himself on the aisle. He was afraid she might panic and run off.

The train started. Nadia was trembling. He took her hand and stared out of the window at the blur of buildings.

They were out of the city and speeding past fields when Nadia turned in her seat.

'He was dead?'

'Yes,' he said. 'I think so.'

'I kill him,' she said, tears in her eyes again.

'No, no.' He put his other hand over hers. 'You didn't mean to. You were protecting me. He'd have killed me. You saved my life.'

'You shall not kill.' She said it as if that was all there was to it.

He hadn't the energy to argue.

'I do,' she said. 'A sin.'

She opened her Bible and began to read.

The farther they got from the city the more frightened he began to feel. The adrenaline, or whatever had kept him going and given him the energy, the clarity of mind, to take action, had drained away.

What am I doing? he asked himself. Why did this happen to me? Why did I go to her room? What am I going to do now?

Doubt weakened him still more.

They reached the station where they had to change trains. He bought coffee and sandwiches for something to do. They drank the coffee but left the sandwiches unopened.

Nadia said she had to go to the toilet. He showed her where it was and used the men's loo himself, then waited outside the ladies'. She took so long he began to fret and was about to go in and find her when she came out. He could see she had been sick. She was deathly pale, with brown rings round her eyes, her lips violently red, and she smelt sour.

They went outside to a seat near the end of the platform well away from other passengers. It was cold but they didn't care. The fresh air was cleansing.

They sat close together holding hands.

He stared down the tracks in the direction their train would come.

The horror of what had happened began to torment him. He needed help. Someone to talk to. Someone who would know what to do. He thought of phoning his father but remembered he was away on business until that evening. His mother would be teaching. He couldn't ring her till after school.

Trains came and went.

The silence between times was cold and heavy.

The minutes passed like hours.

He'd never felt so miserable in his life.

At last they were on their way. Nothing said.

For a few minutes Nadia drifted into sleep but woke when the train stopped at a station.

'Half an hour and we're there,' he said to reassure himself as much as her.

It was after five when they arrived. He thought of ringing his mother to pick them up, but that would mean explaining on the phone and how could he do that in a few minutes without panicking her? Better to walk.

They set off.

They were almost home when they came to a church.

Nadia stopped in front of it and said, 'I kill him.'

He said nothing.

'I confess,' she said.

There was a new determination in her voice.

'Now?' he said. 'It's a Roman Catholic church. Is that your kind?'

'Orthodox,' she said. 'But the priest understand. I must. I am damned if I do not.'

She went to the church door. It was locked.

They went to the presbytery and rang the bell.

An old priest in a shabby black suit and clerical collar opened the door.

Now Nadia couldn't say anything.

'Yes?' the priest said.

'She wants to speak to you,' he managed to say.

'Come in,' the priest said, standing aside.

The hall smelt of polish and dust. The furniture and floor were dark old wood, the strip of carpet was threadbare.

'Wait here,' the priest said to him.

'Come with me,' he said to Nadia.

He waited. There was a picture on the wall. Christ with his bleeding heart. He thought of the man lying dead on the floor. The image made him tremble and break into a cold sweat again. How could anyone like anything so gruesome, he wondered and tried not to look at the picture, but there was nothing else on the walls.

There was a chair under it.

He sat down, feeling lost.

He checked his watch many times before the priest emerged.

He stood up.

The priest looked at him with a wry smile.

'What's your name?' he said.

'Jack Hudson.'

'You live round here? I've seen you sometimes.'

'Yes. Somerset Gardens.'

'Right, Jack Hudson. This is a pretty pickle.'

He nodded.

'Tell me your side of the story.'

When he'd finished, the priest said, 'What were you thinking of doing?'

'Take her home. Ask my parents. I don't know. Maybe she could stay with us. I just don't know.'

He started to feel the same sort of panic as when the agora attacked. Like then, he felt confused, nothing making any sense. But this time there was nowhere to go.

He started to breathe faster and was close to tears.

'Are you a Catholic?' the priest asked.

He shook his head and wiped his eyes and was gasping now.

'Stand up,' the priest said. 'Take three deep breaths. After me. OK? Now . . . one . . . two . . . three.'

He did as he was told. The panic began to subside.

'You're not Catholic. Are you anything? Church of England. Methodist. Any of the mad cults.'

He shook his head again. 'Nothing.'

'No faith at all?'

He burst out, 'I don't know what to do! It's like a nightmare.'

'All right. All right. You're safe here. Try again. Three deep breaths.'

He felt calmer.

'Now listen to me,' the priest said. 'I believe both of you. The girl's confessed and I've absolved her. She's as innocent as the day is long. More sinned against than sinning. She has nothing to answer for. And neither have you. There's no way this poor child can be given up to the authorities without somebody to speak for her. But what she's told me in there is under the seal of the confessional. I can't reveal it to anybody. You understand what I mean?'

'Yes.'

'But what you've told me isn't. So that leaves me free to help, if I can. The trouble is she could be charged with murder, or at best manslaughter. And you could be charged as an accessory. You understand what that means?'

He nodded and sat down.

'There's only one thing I can think to do. Have you ever heard of the law of sanctuary?'

'No.'

'It was a law that said if a fugitive from justice gets to a church he can claim sanctuary, and the law can't touch him while he's in the church. Trouble with it is, the law went out four hundred years ago. But it still has some moral authority. It's been used a few times in recent years to protect people unjustly threatened with deportation. It's not legal. It has no power in law. But it has a lot of power as publicity. Draws the attention of the media. Newspapers, TV, radio. Stirs up public opinion. The authorities don't like that. Not keen on it one bit. Makes them think before acting. Gives us time to prepare a good defence and raise money for it. You see where I'm going?'

'You think Nadia should stay here in the church?'

'Not just her. You as well.'

'Me!'

'It's the only way to protect you.'

'I don't know . . . What about my parents?'

'Right. You and the girl stay here. I'll go and talk to your parents. Bring them here to talk to you and meet the girl. Take it from there. One step at a time. Nobody else needs to know anything yet. You'll be safe here for a while. Then I must contact the police. And get a doctor to look at that poor girl. After what she's been through God knows—'

They looked at each other.

'I was only trying to help,' Jack said.

'Yes, well, you've discovered there's a cost for everything. Even saving somebody.'

The priest glanced at the picture and added, 'Especially saving somebody.'

Jack said, 'I don't know what to do.'

'Go to her,' the priest said. 'You need her now as much as she needed you before.'

He went into the room.

It was dim, smelt of dust and a lingering of what he didn't know was musky incense brought in day after day, year after year, on the priest's clothes after mass and infused into the fabric of the curtains, the ancient furniture and the foot-worn carpet with its faded colours in a flowery design. Holy pictures were on the walls and a large crucifix above the empty fireplace, an old clock ticking on the mantelpiece.

But what he saw was not the surroundings, only Nadia, who stood up as he entered.

She looked clean, as if recently bathed, her eyes bright and her face no longer bleached with worry.

She smiled widely at him.

'Father Thomas absolve me,' she said.

'Good,' he said, but there was no goodness in his voice.

'You do not believe,' she said, the smile gone.

'No.'

She shrugged.

'It is a mystery,' she said, and sat down.

'Too mysterious for me,' he said.

'I'm sorry,' she said.

'What for?'

'You see only on top.'

'On top?'

She waved her hand side to side, as if polishing something.

'You mean the surface?' he said.

'Yes. The surface. You see only the surface. Not under. Under is where all is.'

'Well, thanks.'

'Please. You help me. I thank you. I am dead without you.'

'And you saved me. I don't know about—what you call it?—absolved. But I do know what you did was self-defence and to save me. Isn't that good enough?'

'It is wrong to kill. You did not kill. I kill. I did not want to, but I kill. Killing anyone is a sin. All killing. I have confessed. I repent. Father Thomas absolves me. God forgives me.'

'That's what you believe. All I know is, it's right to save your own life and it's good to save the life of someone else. You did both, and that's all I can say.'

'There is more than you say.'

'I'll take your word for it.'

'One day you find out.'

They contemplated each other, she in the chair, he standing in front of the fireplace.

'You have much to learn,' she said, and smiled.

'About that we agree,' he said. 'But what we both have to learn right now is how we get out of this mess. Because, honestly, I don't think the priest—'

'Father Thomas.'

'—will be able to save us for long. You might think you're absolved or whatever, but, if you ask me, the police won't care about that.'

'Father Thomas knows what to do.'

'I hope you're right.'

'You must trust.'

'Maybe you have too much.'

'I trust you. Why not Father Thomas?'

They looked at each other in silence again.

Until Nadia stood up and said, 'There will be kitchen. I make coffee.'

And went, leaving Jack standing in front of the empty fireplace and the crucified man, waiting for what would happen next, because he could do nothing else.

 Weather forecast

A YOUNG WOMAN AND A YOUNG MAN SITTING *on a bus.*

    Man: It's bad.

Woman: Excuse me?

    Man: The weather. It's bad.

Woman: Oh! Yes. Yes, it is.

(Pause)

    Man: Not as bad as yesterday though.

Woman: No.

    Man: Colder yesterday.

Woman: Was it?

    Man: I had to wear my coat. It's cold today, I thought. I'd better wear my coat.

(Pause)

Woman: It's sunnier today.

    Man: I'm sorry?

Woman: Today. It's sunnier.

Man: Yes. Yes, it is.

Woman: It'll rain though.

Man: You think so?

Woman: It has to. They said it had to. On the telly this morning, they said it had to rain today.

Man: It's bound to. I haven't brought my coat.

(*Pause*)

Man: It's bright enough now though.

Woman: They sometimes get it wrong.

Man: They do.

Woman: They were wrong yesterday. Yesterday they said it would be warm and sunny.

Man: And it was cold and cloudy. That's why I wore my coat.

(*Pause*)

Woman: Mind you, it's not easy. Forecasting.

Man: It's the weather. It's that changeable.

Woman: Me — I just expect what comes.

Man: That's the best way.

Woman: Take what comes. That's how I look at life.

Man: That's the right way.

Woman: Take what life offers.

Man: Me too.

(*Pause*)

Woman: The long-range forecast is awful.

Man: Is it?

Woman: Terrible. A month of cold winds and rain, they said.

Man: On the telly?

Woman: They said it on the telly yesterday.

Man: I missed that.

Woman: They could be wrong.

Man: Life is unpredictable.

Woman: All guesswork.

Man: You can't blame them. With the weather the way it is.

(*Pause*)

Woman: Mind you, I don't think this sun will last.

Man: Nothing does, does it? Not for long.

Woman: Too good to last.

Man: I knew I should have brought my coat.

Woman: Still, got to look on the bright side.

Man: Stay hopeful.

Woman: Take what comes.

(*Pause*)

Woman: I get off here.

Man: Me too.

Something to Tell You

BEN AND NATHALIE ARE STANDING ON A
bridge over a river.

Ben: There's something I have to tell you.

Nat: You're dumping me.

Ben: No!

Nat: You are. You're breaking us up.

Ben: No, that's not it.

Nat: I knew it. You've been different lately.

Ben: No I haven't.

Nat: For the last few weeks.

Ben: No I haven't.

Nat: Yes you have. You've been sort of quiet.

Ben: Because of what I have to tell you.

Nat: You've met somebody else.

Ben: No.

Nat: You have. It's what I've always dreaded.

Ben: It isn't that at all.

Nat: Where did you meet her?

Ben: I haven't met anybody.

Nat: What's her name?

Ben: There isn't anybody.

Nat: Is she blonde or brunette? I bet she's brunette.

Ben: No.

Nat: Not *ginger*, is she? That would be *the worst*.

Ben: No.

Nat: You want a change. That's what it is.

Ben: No, I don't.

Nat: You're bored with me.

Ben: I am *not* bored with you.

Nat: How long have we been going out together?

Ben: What?

Nat: There! You see! You can't remember.

Ben: Eight months. We've been going out for eight months. Eight months next Friday, actually.

Nat: But you had to think about it. Had to work it out, didn't you.

Ben: Listen, Nat.

Nat: I don't need to listen. I can guess the whole story already.

Ben: Please, Nat, listen. There's something I
have to tell you.

Nat: All right. Have it your own way. Really
upset me.

Ben: It's that—

Nat: Tell me all the gory details. Go on.

Ben: My mother.

(*Pause*)

Ben: She's in hospital.

(*Pause*)

Ben: They thought she had cancer.

(*Pause*)

Ben: We were afraid she might die.

(*Pause*)

Ben: That's why I never told you. Didn't
want to upset you.

(*Pause*)

Ben: But they think she's all right. They're
not totally sure. But she's probably OK.
She's coming home tomorrow.

(*Pause*)

Nat: Thank god! I thought you were going to
dump me.

Ben: Excuse me?

Nat: It would've been the end of me. Honestly,
Ben, it would have totally been the end
of me.

Ben: Did you hear what I said?

Nat: Yes. Course I did. And I'm really sorry about your mum. But what a relief!

Ben: Nat!

Nat: I'm here for you, Ben.

(Pause)

Ben: Nat.

Nat: What?

Ben: Go chuck yourself in the river.

Nat: Ben! What's the matter? Ben! Don't walk off like that.

You Can Be Anything

I CAN BE ANYTHING I WANT TO BE I CAN DO anything I want to do I know I can be anything I want to be and I know I can do anything I want to do I know because they tell us that we can be anything we want to be and we can do anything we want to do all we have to do is want to be it enough and want to do it enough and if we want it enough we can be anything we want to be and if we want it enough we can do anything we want to do and as I look out of my window at people passing by in the street like that woman with a baby in a pram I know that the baby will be anything it wants to be and do anything it wants to do as long as it wants to be it enough and wants to do it enough whether it's a boy or a girl or black or white or sky-blue pink because that's what they say.

(Pause)

I want to be a Grand Slam tennis player I want to be a Grand Slam tennis player more than anything else in the world.

(Pause)

Only they don't tell me how I can be a Grand Slam tennis player no matter how much I really want it now that I have no legs which they cut off me after the accident with the car.

(Pause)

Unless they are lying unless they were always lying unless you can't be what you want to be and can't do anything you want to do no matter how much you want to be it and how much you want to do it unless everything else is right and if they are lying all I can be is someone who sits here in this chair with wheels instead of legs and all I can do is look out of my window at the people walking along the street who can be anything they want to be and do anything they want to do.

(Pause)

They wouldn't lie about something as big as that.

(Pause)

Would they?

A Handful of Wheat

THE URGE TO BE A WRITER TOOK HOLD WHEN *I was fifteen. But what should I write about? I knew I wanted to write stories, novels preferably. I'd been told by teachers to write about what I knew. But what do you know when you're only fifteen and live a sheltered, unadventurous life? Other people's lives were interesting. Mine was boring.*

Write about something you feel passionate about, a teacher told me. One event came to mind. The death of my coal-miner grandfather in 1945. I was very fond of him. He took me on walks when I was little, and told me some of the first stories I can remember. His death was a distressing shock. It still upsets me. I was passionate about that. So here it is. I was seventeen when I finished it. It went through many drafts before this one.

All the other stories in this book are about people aged fourteen to seventeen. It seemed fitting to include a story written by someone of that age.

When I was ten my mother's father died. Ever since I can remember until the time he became ill my mother had taken me to see my grandparents on Sunday afternoons. The visits had become a ritual. I would be scrubbed in the kitchen sink until my skin shone, was taut and drum-like. Then I would draw in my breath with a low hiss to show my dislike of the clean woollen socks my mother pulled on, the starched, almost rough grey shirt, stiff grey suit and plastered-down hair. At last I would sit like a life-size china boy waiting for my mother to come downstairs ready to go in her high-heeled court shoes and tight black two-piece costume, which I never liked.

But when Grandad became ill I only visited once. I was afraid of the warm, forbidding air of the sickroom, the wet clamminess of his hands. I shied away from the restrictions his sickness imposed on the household. The forced quietness, the talk about illness, the general air of trouble made me feel that everyone was infected, not just Grandad. The sharp, bitter tang of coal, which used to fill the miner's house, had given way to a warm fetid body-smell.

The news of his death came one night. My mother's eyes reddened and swam in tears, but as soon as she saw my discomfort, my wonder, she tried to brighten up. Even so, I knew it had hurt her and because I knew it would hurt her even more if I did not, I tried to throw off my fear and promised to go with her to see Grandma.

The next day was Sunday. The normality of the routine ritual helped me to pretend there was nothing really wrong. But still, I was more cooperative over washing and dressing, and Mother was more gentle than usual with the hateful clean socks and best Sunday clothes.

We left the house. Dad was digging in the back garden sullen with guilt because he knew he should be coming too, but wouldn't. He never did come with us on these Sunday visits, I never knew why and never asked. It was a damp autumn day, cold despite the sun, with spongy yellow leaves making the road like sodden old blotting paper. We walked down the road carrying the day like pallbearers by the side of the treacly river we called The Burn, that carried away the sulphurous refuse of a coke factory which smoked all day and fumed all night at the head of the valley. The day seemed like a yellow, wet, washed-out watercolour.

There were not many passengers waiting for the bus, but the main street crawled with Sunday crowds. Their bobbing heads suddenly seemed ridiculous like rebel jack-in-the-boxes. And all of them, except one or two dusty pitmen just off their shift, who lounged around a pub door, were got up to kill in their once-a-week clothes. Between the banks of people the road was almost deserted but for an occasional car, the odd bus, and a stray dog that seemed to prefer the risk of being squashed by the traffic to the dangerous feet on the pavement. It was a relief when our bus arrived to drag my mother upstairs, from where I could look down on the people below, all heads and shoulders. I felt comfortable and removed peering at them, and wondered if that's how it felt when you were dead.

Grandad was dead. Perhaps he was chuckling as he looked down on us. He used to sit at one end of the table in the living room and drum on top of the table with his fingers. He never sat in an easy chair. He used to sit easy in the fields though. 'Sit easy, son, sit easy, and if th' canny sit easy, sit as easy as th' can.' That was when he used to take me for walks round the fields to get an appetite for tea and to get me out of the house so that my grandma and six aunts and my mother could gossip without me overhearing. But in the summer I never got my appetite because we used to rub the heads of ripe corn in our hands, blow the chaff away and eat the little nuts. And always, once a summer, Grandad used to pick a bunch of ripe corn and hang it upside down from a rusty nail behind the back door, because it was supposed to bring good luck. This year he hadn't been out for any because he was ill in bed. And this year Grandad died.

We got off the bus at the bottom of the valley on the edge of the mining village where my grandparents lived and my mother had grown up. We walked up the hill past the rows of terrace houses built of stone, which had turned a dull crumbly black. The streets were long, thick, solid things that seemed to squat because of their chunky length, like great brooding animals. Regularly along their front sides were two windows and a door, two windows and a door, two windows and a door, a monotonous procession. I let my hand *clap clap clap* along the wooden railings at the ends of the gardens until a jagged edge nicked my finger. I walked on, sucking my injured hand.

One or two of the men and their wives who were working in their gardens or squatting on the doorsteps nodded to my mother and gave a slight, half-pitying smile, as people do who want to be sympathetic, knowing there has been a death, but none of them spoke.

When we came to the row where my grandparents lived we turned into the back lane. The backs of the houses faced each other, each house with its walled yard and outbuildings equally divided into coalhouse and dry lavatory. The lane was gritty and hard. Our shoes crunched at every step, a weak echo walking along with us. Children were screaming round a flyblown ice-cream van, which occasionally let off a cacophony of motor-horn blasts. Some of the children stared blankly at me because of my clothes and I could feel them leering at me, then laughing and scoffing when we were past.

We reached Grandma's and swung into the back-yard without a pause, trying to hide our apprehension and nervousness.

The back door led straight into the big kitchen/living room. The curtains were drawn over the one window that looked out onto the backyard. The room was shrouded in the suffused light. As we entered, Mother first, me behind clinging to her hand, I saw the arc of quiet women sitting round the black-leaded range. Their heads turned to look at us.

'Here she is!' cried Aunty Doris, pretending cheerfulness. 'We were just saying you'd come today.'

I liked Doris, my favourite aunt. She was playful and never bad-tempered or cross. She had a bulbous pear-drop nose I always laughed at.

The arc opened, another chair was brought for my mother, and a little stool for me was placed between her and Doris. I was pleased; it meant I would not be stuck up in the air but could hide among the knees. Grandma was at the end of the group, enthroned in the corner against the wall in her big armchair and robed in a copious pink shawl. She looked up now for the first time.

'Aye, I knew she'd come,' she said quietly, not at all in her usual gay, high-pitched voice.

Mother went to her, stepping over the legs in the way, and kissed her.

'And my bonny lad,' Grandma said.

But I couldn't move. The pallid face, the great old body filling the chair were unapproachable. They repelled me, made a sour taste invade my mouth. I could only mutter, 'Hello, Grandma.'

Everyone settled down again. The fire flickered and blustered in its deep well; the bellicose kettle, crusted with soot, puffed and fumed on the grate. Everyone stared at it. There were two stout greying women in the arc, wearing limp black dresses and stained pinafores. They kept looking round, especially at Grandma, with slow, alert eyes. They seemed to be waiting to catch anything that was said or done like fat vultures. I didn't like them and wondered why they were there.

'Who's got the funeral?' my mother asked suddenly.

The eyes of the two vultures swivelled round; my aunts moved, grateful for the break into conversation.

'Man from Seggison,' said Grandma tonelessly, grudgingly.

'Lovely man,' said one of the old women. 'Did Mrs. Bains a wonderful job.'

'Aye!' agreed the other, drawing in her breath.

'Looked beautiful did Mr. Bains. Better than when he was alive, poor man.'

'He's none so bad,' Grandma condescended. 'He gave our Elsie a nice send-off anyway.'

I wondered what a 'nice send-off' was. I tried to remember Great Aunt Elsie's. It had had a lot of flowers. Perhaps that was a nice send-off? I thought of the pale wooden coffin and the men lowering it slowly into the grave. It seemed so heavy, yet when the vicar said, 'Earth to earth, ashes to ashes . . .' and the man from Sacriston had thrown soil in a shower onto the coffin, it had sounded hollow and empty. I imagined Great Aunt Elsie had got out, that only the empty box had been lowered into the grave, that she would come and frighten us all at tea after her nice send-off, when everyone was looking relieved and were overanxiously pleasant because of the relief. But she had not, and now she was a mound of grassy earth in a chapel yard, a few faded flowers bowing their shrivelled heads over her middle.

'Poor lad, he's gone now,' Grandma moaned.

My aunts shuffled uneasily, wondering what to say.

'Aye, and I treated him badly, you know.'

She lifted a crumpled, freckled hand to support her bottom lip.

'Now, Mother, no you didn't,' said Aunty May. She was the youngest, still in her twenties, thin and belligerent. 'He often said things to you that nobody would have put up with.' She turned her head away from us.

'Maybe maybe,' Grandma said slowly and vaguely, not taken in by her daughter. 'But he was a good man all the same, and he only ever give back what I threw at him.'

There was a silence. I wanted to move a leg that was going to sleep but daren't, for I knew if I did someone would notice and speak to me in hope of changing the conversation.

'Ah, why! Th's looked after him well since he's been ill,' said one of the flabby women at last, making a compromise between the two parties.

'Aye, but there was a time when I threw him out of the house. Nor, and he didn't get back in for three weeks.'

Grandma was chuckling now, with a smile on her face, her massive round shoulders jerking up and down. She might have been crying tearlessly but for the sharpness of her eyes, a sharpness that made me wither up and hug myself.

'Well anyhow, he went wi' out any bother,' the woman said in a last effort to please.

'He did an' all,' said Grandma, sobered. 'Aye, gone home, the lad has. And me none so far behind, God willing.' She shook her head, her eyes fixed on her knees, as though part of her was already on its way.

'Now, Mother, there's no need for that kind of talk,' my mother said, getting up and putting the kettle on the fire. 'Come on, Doris, we'll get some tea.'

Chairs were pushed back, my aunts stood up, skirts were pulled down and straightened, shoes put on. The straining snugness poured away like pressure from a tube when the valve is released. I felt I could move and breathe again. Doris and Mary went off into the pantry, my mother and May began laying the table.

'Dear me, tea time already!' sang one of the neighbor women, peering exorbitantly at the alarm clock clacking on the mantelpiece, and finally slapping her knees before rising.

'I suppose we'll have to be away,' said the other woman.

'Now don't you worry yourself, missus.' the first bent over Grandma. 'Don't bother yourself.' She was almost bellowing her advice into Grandma's ear, determined to let everyone hear. 'Your daughters look after you, and if you want owt just let's know and our Jim can get it.' She patted Grandma's shoulder, said, 'Tarra,' and followed by her companion left the house to calls of 'Thank you, Mrs. Clayton, tarra.'

The house sank into its funereal silence. The low tones of Doris and Mary murmuring in the scullery and the clinking of cups as the table was set made me aware of myself. I was alone, with Grandma still brooding in her corner. Terror flooded up my spine. I saw her like a great eagle, peering in the bold, wide-eyed, impersonal way of the eagle, far into the fire. And I was sure that if she turned her eyes upon me she would pounce as the eagle would and use me as her prey. I shivered. Sweat prickled on my brow and between my shoulders. My stomach palpitated, hot and afraid. Getting up, I darted into the scullery, thinking to escape by pretending to help Doris. She was swathing thick slices of bread with layers of butter and arranging them on a plate. Mary was leaning against the table, arms folded.

Doris caught me by the shoulder and pulled me between them.

'Now listen, love,' she half whispered. 'Your grandmother's not well, you know, because Grandad's dead. So don't make a nuisance of yourself, there's a good lad.' She waved the buttery knife at me and held up the plate of bread. 'Here, take this to your mother.'

I took the plate and went back into the room. As I made towards the table I took a quick look at Grandma. She was as I had left her, well back in her chair, her arms splayed along the chair's arms, her eyes devouring the fire. My mother smiled, wanting to brighten me up, but too busy with preparations to do more. I was left feeling stranded and insecure in the middle of the room.

The garden came as a thought in salvation. I had opened the door into the front room on my way to the front door before I remembered that Grandad would be there in his coffin. And there it was, a long seam of creamy wood, its open top gaping at the ceiling, white satin frothing over the edge. A dull, sweet, unhealthy smell spiced with disinfectant was thick in the air. And Grandad's waxen face was visible above the coffin's rim, his head resting on a white cushion.

I tasted the foul air clogging my mouth. Half turning to flee back into the living room, I knew I couldn't. Casting my eyes down and holding my breath, I ran to the front door and, once outside, banged it behind me.

I walked slowly down the garden path, trembling and breathing rapidly now. At each breath the fear and tension in my body slipped further away. My eyes began to see the grey afternoon, the long black mounds of houses, the roses beginning to shed their discoloured petals, the long knife-leaves and blue flowers of the gladioli my grandma loved so much.

The breeze cooled the sweat on my body. The trembles of fear ran into cold shivers.

At the bottom of the garden, among the cabbages and potatoes, I kicked myself onto the top of the gate, and sat, legs swinging, looking back at the house. It seemed like a slice in the long burnt loaf of the terrace, the windows blinded by drawn curtains. I stared at the downstairs window, thinking of Grandad in his coffin, stiff, his skin putty-coloured, the grey wisps of his hair combed neatly to one side, his tobacco-stained moustache neatly trimmed, his face quiet, removed, aloof.

I was suddenly possessed by the realisation that age and death would come to me too. The thought left me feeling as though purged by acid, somehow clear, aware of every sensation, aware of breathing, the movement of my eyes, the very act of seeing, aware of my hair, my ears, my mouth, my teeth, the saliva in my mouth, my bowels, my legs swinging and banging against the gate, my clothes chafing against my skin, and my hands gripping the top of the gate.

There was nothing about me at that moment that I did not know. And the knowledge was an unbearable pain.

Slipping to my feet, I shook my head violently, hanging onto the gate for support. The grains of the wood, worn to ridges by the weather, dug into my fingers. I could think of nothing but those sharp, thin furrows and the whole fullness of the wood under my hands. I concentrated on them. They seemed such a pure, undemanding, unfailing comfort.

A Note from the Author about Flash Fiction

Several of the stories in this collection are a kind that are now called flash fictions. Along with many writers, I've become more and more interested in them as a modern form that is at the cutting edge of literature. This is what I like about them:

They are like a flash of light, a spark, which allows one quick view of a whole scene or person or event.

They are usually less than 1,000 words long.

They can be of any genre so long as they are stories.

They can be autobiography, biography, poems, letters, diaries, mini essays, news reports. . .

They can be prose with or without dialogue, or only dialogue.

They can be in the first person, or third person, and in any tense.

In other words, they can make use of any aspect of language and written expression.

They must be complete, and not a mere anecdote.

They often leave as much for the reader to do, making the story, and "making the meaning," as the author does.

They have a neatness and a rhythm that are apparently simple but, when you think about them, you realize are very dense and full of possible meanings.

Some of the greatest authors of literature wrote flash fictions. For example, Kafka, Chekhov, Hemingway, Raymond Carver, Italo Calvino, and Kawabata, which he called "palm-of-the-hand" stories.

One of the reasons why they are so popular and are such a very modern kind of literature is that they are suited to writing and reading on the small screens of computers, iPhones, and eReaders.

I hope you enjoy them as much as I do.

—Aidan Chambers